Astrid Beeswax

The Venom

Author: Tessa Jensen
Illustrator: Lizzy D. Hill

1

Paperback ISBN: 979-8-9858326-6-2
eBook ISBN: 979-8-9858326-7-9

First paperback edition

Proofread by Suzanne Duvall
Cover art and illustrations by Lizzy D. Hill

tessa-jensen.com

Table of Contents

CURRENT AFFAIRS......................................7

ROLAND'S STRUGGLE AND MILLIE RUMOROUS 18

HAROLD AND FREDERICK 39

LOVE PREPARED FOR THE HEARTACHE 53

REGARDING PRISCILLA.............................70

TRUTH SPECTACLES.................................83

OSWALD, MR. PIP, AND OLD GRIEVANCES......................................105

THE EASTER BRUNCH 123

MR. PIP'S CONCERNS 160

OPHELIA PAYNE 169

MAMA'S LOVE AND PRISCILLA'S JOURNAL................................ 187

THE BUNCO GAME.. 196

FIRE AND A ROLLS ROYCE PHANTOM .. 217

THE TRACK MEET 229

ABOUT THE AUTHOR 244

ABOUT THE ILLUSTRATOR 245

Dedicated to

Eli and Elliott

Current Affairs

Forgiveness wrought a profound transformation within Astrid Beeswax, which you will soon learn. Yet, let there be no mistake: she remained the quintessential creative force behind The Bee's Knees, a haven renowned for its exquisite floral arrangements gracing elite gatherings and citywide events. Rooted in her adoration for the Vintage American 1950s aesthetic, Astrid's signature style manifested in meticulously coordinated ensembles of dresses, hats, and accessories that captivated onlookers. With ears finely attuned to the world around her, she continued intercepting a symphony of sound waves that the average ear could not hear, gathering the most lucrative of all assets, other people's business. Astrid's floral creations occasionally concealed discreet bumble bee listening devices to capitalize on her opportunities, granting Astrid access to conversations beyond her physical reach.

Astrid and her bosom friend, Lottie Dah, originally devised the bumble bee scheme with a singular

aim: to dismantle Harold Braggart, the charismatic tycoon whose actions led to her father's demise and her mother's blindness years earlier. Astrid's triumph, however, unveiled the true architect behind Harold's malevolent deeds. Adelaide Braggart, the callous matriarch of the Braggart dynasty, reveled in orchestrating a labyrinth of deceit and manipulation within the hockey-obsessed city of Doily Dayle. Tasking Harold with scapegoating Astrid's brother, Roland, head coach of Moose University's hockey team, Adelaide's intricate facade crumbled spectacularly. Driven by deep-seated animosity towards his mother, Harold, while doing his mother's bidding, meticulously amassed a dossier of incriminating evidence: financial records, clandestine transactions, hush-money agreements, illicit trades, and photographic proof. When the final hand was played, Adelaide could no longer deny her complicity in instructing her then-teenage son to ignite the fatal blaze within the fireworks tent where Astrid's parents were preparing for Doily Dayle's Harvest Festival spectacle.

To those who believe money compensates for the insurmountable deficit of motherly love and affection, Harold appeared to benefit from Adelaide's selfishness. He became the youngest-ever athletic director of Moose University, and his last name ensured that when he spoke, his words became gospel to the many devoted sports fans who were more devoted to their gods than many a Christian in a pew.

There was no shortage of people willing to do him a favor and no upscale event where he was not one of the first on the guest list. The intoxication of fame and power had a potent effect on Harold, and if one pretends to be someone long enough, even for a good purpose, pretending becomes no longer necessary.

To complicate Harold's emotional tightrope walk, he had been fascinated with Astrid since their first encounter. He had fallen on the ground after his skateboard hit a strategically placed rock, and she appeared conveniently as the picture of grace, handed him a piece of chocolate-dipped biscotti while wearing a Kelly-green gingham dress, a sunny yellow bowler hat and black patent Mary Janes. They had been twelve, and she had disliked him instantly.

However, Astrid spent years encouraging his flirtations in the name of vanity and revenge, and her pretending was equally compromising. In the end, when the swirling debris of interpersonal and public disaster abated and the truth was fully known, the two maintained a friendly correspondence.

At this juncture of ongoing repairs of mind and heart, we return to our story of Astrid Beeswax. Her next set of adventures will prove far more challenging than the first.

***

Spring had descended upon Doily Dayle with such humility that most citizens were still lamenting the winter, which was undoubtedly, they insisted, three months longer than the previous year. Astrid was never taken by surprise, for with her magnificently sharp hearing she was the first to hear the birds' songs. The American Robin, with its cheerful melody, announced the arrival of new life and new blooms. The Song Sparrow, Mourning Dove, and Red-winged Blackbird joined in the chorus, and Astrid hummed a playful tune to sing along.

In jubilant homage to the flourishing season, The Bee's Knees metamorphosed into a resplendent symphony of hues, where shades of pink, purple, white, and yellow danced harmoniously across the tiled floor, up the windows, and hung from the ceiling like the aerial acrobatics of a trapeze artist. Astrid spent hours and days meticulously curating a vintage array of porcelain vases, each cradling long-stemmed tulips, happy and bright daffodils, jovial daisies, and enchanting lilies. Amidst this botanical symphony, the fragrant whispers of lilacs and hyacinths wafted through the air, infusing the space with their can-never-be-bottled perfume. At the same time, white wicker baskets overflowed with pastel roses, their delicate petals rejoicing in bloom.

"Ah, springtime!" Astrid exclaimed with a contented sigh, savoring the fresh morning air. Our florist donned a charming full-swing dress to celebrate the season and elevate her mood,

drawing inspiration from the delicate purple wisteria vines.

The fitted bodice, crafted from silk crepe de chine in a serene wisteria lavender, was adorned with intricately embroidered flower motifs in icy lilac and indigo shades. A row of petite fabric-covered buttons trailed down to the cinched waistline along the graceful V-shaped neckline at the back. The skirt, flowing in a circular silhouette, came in layers of sky blue and wisteria-hued tulle, reminding Astrid of many a childhood Easter dress. An oversized amethyst sash cinched her slender waist and satisfied her long-held belief that bows chase away melancholy because they felt like a hug. Completing her ensemble, Astrid adorned herself with a wide-brimmed golden straw sun hat accented with a matching amethyst sash, white suede t-strap pumps, and subtle yet elegant pearl earrings.

The rays of sunshine buoyed her spirits. In many ways, a personal winter had settled into her soul since January, after the hope and anticipation of Christmas and the lights of the new year faded and the wrapping and tissue paper thrown away. The absence of her two social anchors had been nigh unbearable. Her twin brother, Roland, and her best friend, Lottie, spent their time almost exclusively together, as newlyweds often do, and Astrid was left to herself. Well, not entirely to herself. She still lived with her angelic mother, Beatrice. Nova Flaherty, the Fire Child who lived next door with Astrid's beloved and retired friend, Mr. Pip,

frequented her driveway and The Bee's Knees as often as her seven-year-old schedule allowed. Which is to say, nearly every day.

Astrid enjoyed the regular stream of familiar clients, and while she was ever full of opinions and anecdotes, she kept the tenderness of her heart to herself. Knowing that no topic interests most people more than themselves, Astrid asked more questions and answered fewer. Please do not misunderstand. Astrid was not angry or defensive; she was aware of the response when she was deemed too much. Too loud. Too intense. Too ambitious. Too demanding. Too dramatic. The taking up of too much psychological space. Nervous smiles, the biting of lower lips as conversation participants shifted their eyes between themselves, and the sudden urgency to attend a feigned appointment or use the restroom pricked her heart as if someone had wrapped a quilt around it with hundreds of sewing pins still attached.

After the events of the previous fall, she didn't have the emotional capital to process the body language or the comments when they came. So she remained socially aloof, which, to her chagrin, was only viewed as supportive evidence of her too much-ness. Additionally, she had started receiving a steady stream of unwelcome letters either left on her car windshield, near the cash register, or in her home mailbox. Each letter was written on vintage stationery in handwriting that mimicked her father's, was signed with his name, and sealed with

the Beeswax seal. She started calling them the Backhanded Compliment Collection, and they were more emotionally devastating than she cared to admit.

Alas, Astrid's heart was never intended to draw inward, so she fought against the inclination with all her might, but, some days, she wondered how much she might have left. Thus, when Roland and Lottie said they would stop for a visit, she felt the immediate lift that one expression of love can give.

***

"Roland! Lottie! Happy Spring! Oh, how I have missed your frequent company," said Astrid as she greeted the couple at the door. She gave Roland a side hug before stepping back and taking a complete inventory of his appearance. His black, curly hair was disheveled as usual; he wore straight and relaxed jeans, a titanium ring on his left hand, a black sling around his right shoulder, tattered black Converse tennis shoes, and a smile that did not quite reach his emerald eyes.

"I'm sorry I have been unresponsive to your texts recently," Roland said, rubbing the back of his neck.

"No explanation needed; how are you recovering from your reconstructive clavicle surgery now that a few weeks have passed?" Astrid asked.

"Not well," Lottie volunteered. "However, he has helped me perfect the bumblebees. Because he was

forced to sit on the couch for longer than he ever has in his life, he took up doing puzzles . . ."

Roland gave a sharp nod in agreement. "Not well at all. Because of my broken collarbone I cannot play hockey, run, lift weights, swim, ride a mountain bike, or do anything besides pedal a stationary bike. I've never been so immobile in my life, and I hate every minute of sunshine that I cannot enjoy. The birds are singing, the flowers are blooming, new bark is being laid out in the parks, and all I get to do is . . ."

"Spend time with your wife!" interrupted Lottie as she put her beach-sized teal polka-dot bag on the counter. "As I was telling Astrid, because you had to sit still, I sat still long enough to concentrate because I wanted to be with you. Plus, your entire body cringed when I put on a romantic comedy, so my usual distraction was no longer an option. So, Astrid, because of Roland's unintentional support, my bumblebee improvements are as follows: increased long-range transmission to enable you to hear from further distances, encryption protocols to prevent unauthorized access should the bees ever be intercepted, and noise reduction algorithms to allow for easier concentration on conversations. What do you think?" Lottie asked as she handed Astrid one of the new bees. "One last detail: I bedazzled the bees! How fun is that?"

"Golly gee, Lottie! Your security improvements are brilliant. We cannot be so proud as to think we do not need to take precautionary measures, though I occasionally like to think that we are so brilliant no one could possibly keep up," Astrid said.

"Do you have any upcoming events with our favorite secret-keeping society where we can test them out?" Lottie asked with a playful glint in her eyes as she found a seat on Roland's lap.

"Millie Rumorous is hosting her annual Easter brunch. She telephoned this morning, informing me that I can expect her to place her order in person today," Astrid replied.

"Please forgive my selfishness, ladies. Here I have been feeling sorry for myself for an injury that will soon be a memory while your bumblebees, on the other hand, have unlimited possibilities," Roland said as he planted a tender kiss on Lottie's forehead, realizing again what a devoted and brilliant wife he had and silently chastising himself for his behavior.

"Don't you dare start beating yourself up over having had a few hard weeks. For once, you get to be supported. Take it only as evidence of my love for you," Lottie said, kissing Roland on the cheek. "Astrid, I'm leaving Roland with you while I walk down to the Bloated Solution for fizzy drinks and cookies. I'll pick up your usual order: one peach soda and one giant sugar cookie with extra pink frosting. In exchange, please cheer up our cheerleader."

"I am most happy to oblige," Astrid said. "If you

want to peruse any sales between here and there, take all the time you need. And, if you happen by Stardust Silhouettes, let me know if you see anything I might like.""I'll send a text if I do; I love you both!" Lottie said as she drew her oversized, white-framed aviators over her eyes and walked out.

"Bye!" Roland and Astrid said in unison.

Roland! Lottie! Happy Spring! Oh, how I have missed your frequent company!

Roland's Struggle and Millie Rumorous

"You do not need to speak as if you are at a babysitting job. I might have an injury and more restrictions than I care to admit, but I am still a grown man," Roland said, his resolve to be less grumpy faltering.

"Since we've established that we are both grown adults rather than ungrown adults, pray tell the matters plaguing your mind?" Astrid asked. "And don't consider telling me nothing is wrong and I have nothing to worry about. We shared the same womb and I know you as well as I know myself."

"Fair enough, consider the idea unconsidered. To start, I am tired," Roland said.

"Of?" Astrid asked as she put her hands on her hips, tilted her head, and waited for a forthcoming confession.

"I don't know, Astrid. This obnoxious sling grates on my nerves, as does caring more than others while being accused of not caring. The revolving door conversations plague me, and the injury exacerbates even the slightest annoyance because my emotional capacity is devoted to pain management. Carlisle, Rex, and I have been hard at work organizing the details for a unique sort of track meet. We're calling it the Race Together meet, and having the hockey players help youth experiencing physical disabilities who might otherwise not be able to participate in such an event. The players will push, pull, or carry their buddies through the race so they truly are racing together." Roland said, clenching and unclenching his fists.

"During my last meeting, I was told I was being selfish by requesting more funds to equip the track meet with the luxuries top-performing collegiate athletes enjoy. I asked for quality uniforms and proper footwear for all participants, branded with their names and the Moose University logo. Rex suggested vendors with food and gear, and Carlisle added massage therapists for post-race recovery for any participating athlete who wants one."

"Believe me, Roland, you are not one to hoard selfishness. If that is truly their intent, those who dare cast aspersions upon your compassion and ambition are utterly ignorant of your character and pure intentions. Furthermore, how are you being selfish by requesting the very amenities that are standard for the hockey team?" Astrid insisted, her ire flaring up at the idea that anyone would insult her brother.

Roland scoffed, "I was told that the Race Together track meet is not the same as a sanctioned collegiate sport and that if I want positive publicity to bolster my career, I should find it another way. I explained that my requests are intended to create the celebrated athlete experience for youth who may not otherwise have an opportunity. They deserve to feel valued and needed just like anybody else."

"How did Moose University not understand where you are coming from, and why wouldn't they be on board with such a philanthropic endeavor as it would show that they care about giving back to their devoted community?" Astrid asked.

"Money, priorities, and setting a precedent they have no desire to sustain, I imagine. Because we have had a lackluster season, the university can easily accuse me of selfish motives to justify their decision," Roland explained.

"I imagine Adelaide is still the university's puppet master, and I don't think she likes you, so I would surmise that this battle might only get steeper. How many weeks until the track meet?" Astrid asked.

"A few weeks, and so far we have a track, some folding tables, and ribbons, which are great, but I wanted more for our participants.

"Additionally, I want the hockey team to learn the joy of thinking outside themselves and to know the human resources and money that go into creating their experiences.

"Perhaps I am being selfish. I don't know. Do you know how hard it is to remain quiet when you are accused of possessing the very quality you abhor and have worked a lifetime to overcome, recent behavior notwithstanding?" Roland asked, nodding toward his arm.

"The art of silence has been imparted upon me, though I am yet a student and far from a master. Navigating human interactions is like playing a game where the rules are ever shifting. Do you believe that your team thinks mostly of themselves?"

"Unfortunately, yes. Furthermore, I believe the fans, the athletic department, parents, analyzers, and announcers support the mentality. These grown men, these legal adults, come to me, claiming dissatisfaction with their performance, and instead of taking ownership, they start making suggestions on what other people can do to fix their problem."

"I thought the Moose won nearly every game?" Astrid asked. "Isn't season success measured in games won?"

 Roland unloaded with the intensity Astrid had only seen him exhibit on the ice, "Partly, but the

truth is we played beneath our potential this year. My team members say, 'Coach, I want to get better.' Then I say, 'Put in the work.' They say, 'I already work hard.' I say, 'If you are not willing to work like a champion, you will never be a champion.'

"Then follows their predictable pattern of blaming me for not understanding or being sensitive to their plight—as if my perspective controls their actions and if I were to wave a wand over their head and sprinkle a generous dose of talent dust, they would magically become first in the NHL draft and an instant Hall of Fame inductee.

"When I offer evidence that contradicts their assertion, one or more of the following rationales pours forth: I have loads of schoolwork; the car my parents bought for me is in the shop and getting repaired at their expense; I'm stressed; I need a break; I'm anxious; I'm depressed; I don't feel like waking up earlier; I can't be bothered to learn from someone who knows more than I do because I might get embarrassed; I might get an overuse injury; my favorite show is on; and, the death of all ambition: it's too hard.

"With that approach, they have already decided how far they will advance. They build and install their stop sign before merging on the freeway of possibilities, and somehow, it all comes back to my fault. I tell each recruit that our team is one of high love and high expectations, and they act as if high love equals no expectations. Astrid, before you lecture me on true greatness, I am not suggesting that an impressive hockey career is the pinnacle of a well-lived life.

I am merely saying that the lack of connection between goal and work is infuriatingly astounding. Should I push hard, I'm called unkind. They think I am an ogre if I point directly to where they can improve instead of dancing around the issue.

"What does speaking the truth mean anymore if doing so is so offensive as to render a perfectly able-minded and able-bodied adult to a skulking shadow whose first concern is their personal comfort and convenience? Why is telling an inquiring mind that their current choices are not going to produce their desired future the absence of compassion?"

She was relieved to hear that she was not alone in balancing care and involvement, and she chose her following words carefully. "I suppose building a bridge of understanding might begin with what those accusing you of a lack of compassion understand compassion to mean. One synonym for compassion is pity, and another is leniency. Soft-heartedness, love, and concern are on the other side of the compassion synonym pendulum. So, by speaking straight forward, you show compassion for their long-term benefit. No one needs to feel sorry for another person or themselves because life requires effort. If leniency must be had, let it come in praise and encouragement, not standards of excellence," Astrid said as she placed a frosty glass of lemonade in front of Roland before sitting across from him.

"Would they prefer I not care? Coddle them? Play the game for them? Their life is theirs, not mine," Roland said as the red from held-back tears swirled with the emerald green of his eyes, making stormy clouds charged with thunderbolts.

"If you didn't care, you wouldn't be Roland, so that option is off the table," Astrid said.

"The energy required to stay calm, smile, take no offense, brush it off, save it for the game, and stay unattached has become unbearable," Roland complained, resting one long leg on the knee of the other. "If mediocrity is what they want, then my hands are tied. They would find their time better used if they brought their grievances to the person in the mirror."

"What tipped the apple cart?" Astrid asked.

"Nothing but another conversation in which I ended up expressing an opinion that was neither wanted nor helpful," Roland said as he tried to interlace his fingers out of habit but gave an irritated grunt as he remembered his physical restrictions.

"Do you often have such conversations? You've never mentioned any of them before," observed Astrid.

"I have them almost daily, and I do not mention

them because I will end up ranting as I am doing now, which is no more helpful than the complaints I am complaining about. Between social media and obstructed views from all sides, I am about ready to cancel Race Together entirely. I feel like a monster is raging within myself, escalating the situation. So, I shall sew my lips shut, listen, and ask if someone wants my opinion before volunteering words I will surely regret later," Roland confessed. "However, if I take a deep breath and practice gratitude, I can be grateful for Adelaide's absence. Ethics aside, her personality was nearly impossible to work with."

Astrid raised her eyebrow. "She cultivated a personality like that by design because it gave her what she wanted: control. Are you truly ready to cancel Race Together? Isn't giving your professional opinion part of your job? Don't most sports movies include a coach who says what his or her athletes do not want to hear but are later thankful for the push? From what you told me, you are doing precisely what you were hired to do: create a winning team full of leaders. Others cannot see as far or dream as high as you do. I wouldn't forfeit my long-term vision to save anyone the discomfort of their self-imposed myopia."

Roland took a deep breath and drew a smile in the condensation on the side of his glass of iced lemonade with his thumb. "What is the latest with The Bee's Knees?"

"If you must evade my question, you might do so without such an abrupt turn of conversation," Astrid said as she smoothed her dress, spun on her heel, picked up her watering can and headed toward the casement window to water her purple pansies.

"We have a regular stream of incoming and outgoing orders if that's what you are asking. I create new arrangements, work on my glitter roses, book events, and entertain plans for a second location, but the truth is, I am a bit bored."

"Bored? I have never known you to be bored. You are an expert at creating jobs for yourself: letter writing, book reading, and baking cookies for people who are having a hard day," said Roland.

"Yes, bored. Lonely, if you must know. But my loneliness is my problem, not yours. I have heard oddities amidst the comings and goings of The Bee's Knees that suggest Adelaide has returned," Astrid said before putting her left hand on her waist and squinting her eyes at a mark on the back wall. "And surely I must stop saying 'my loneliness' as if I own and define myself by it. Is that a water stain?"

"Is what a water stain," Roland asked as he turned his body, following Astrid's pointer finger.

She made a beeline for the watermark, placed her watering can on the ground, and pressed her ear to the wall.

"What do you hear?" Roland asked.

"Drip. Drip. Drip. I have a leaking water pipe. Golly gee, I had other plans for my savings account, but leaking water pipes cannot be ignored. I should remove the money from my savings account, put the old germ-covered green bills in a pile, and lit it aflame for the tens of thousands of dollars I have spent on repairs, and that's the final bill after your free labor," Astrid lamented.

"You did inherit Grammy Beeswax's old chocolate shop as the location of The Bee's Knees; unfortunately, old buildings are not known for their efficiency. If you must spend money, and I must spend time every once in a while, to keep everything in working order, it's worth the investment. Plus, we get to spend time together, huh?" Roland said, suddenly cheering up.

"I suppose," Astrid said, surveying the wall. Annoyed, she began removing the décor from the wall: an oval-framed black-and-white picture of her parents in their younger years, one of her Grammy Beeswax with ten-year-old Aloysius and his sister Priscilla, and a floating bookshelf full of handmade gifts from her clients. As she removed the hardware, something about the other side of the wall caught her eye. She rocked forward, back, and forward again, closing one eye and then the other.

"Did you just take notice of the uneven wall?" Roland asked. "If so, it's irreparable. I remember

helping Dad patch it years ago. We spent hours trying to smooth it out, but he said whatever was causing the issue couldn't be removed. When you cannot do anything, you might as well let it go."

"I suppose you're correct, but something looks off about the way it looks off, much like the complete disappearance of Adelaide Braggart, which I will repeat ad nauseam.

I don't believe that there is nothing wrong with this wall any more than I believe that she made a graceful exit from Doily Dayle and intends never to return," Astrid said, still cocking her head from one side to the other as the examined the offending wall from different angles.

"Don't you think you would be less stressed if you weren't paranoid about her return? You can't do anything about her location anyway," Roland said.

Astrid swiveled her head to give her brother a severe but playful glare followed by several slow blinks of her eyelids, "There you go saying 'you can't' again, which sounds like a slogan from the defeatist camp. To clarify, I'm not paranoid; I am realistic. Someone like her does not act alone. She needed associates, people she bribed or threatened, and resources she could not have accumulated otherwise. Adelaide put her own son, Harold, as the head of her evil empire, but he's no longer part of the equation. She would never forfeit her role as the neck that controls the head, so I have been keeping a keen eye for the new face of evil. A face that looks sweet, old, and unassuming, someone the opposite of handsome and determined," Astrid mused.

"Are you now suspicious of every sweet lady and old man in the area?" Roland asked.

"Oh, golly gee, no. Not everyone, just some of them," Astrid said as the bell on the front door jingled, announcing the arrival of a customer.

With a smooth of her dress and a spin on her heel, Astrid greeted the pleasantly plucky and plump Millie Rumorous, the upper-crust purveyor of gossip, age sixty-eight, with curly silver hair fashioned in a fuzzy circle around her head, royal blue polyester pants with a high elastic waist, a bluebird hued cardigan with daisies embroidered around the hem and the ends of the sleeves, with over-sized ocean blue buttons, dolphin earrings, and blue eyeshadow inspired by a 1980s Glamor Shot.

"Hello, Millie!" Astrid exclaimed with an outstretched hand. "I am happy to see you. How is your cat? I trust she remains in excellent health?"

"Puddles remains above ground," Millie Rumorous confirmed with a chuckle and a smile. "You know, I was just at Oswald's Tiny Toys choosing a gift for my nephew's birthday. He's turning eighteen, and I asked Oswald if he and Mr. Pip were talking again. It's been nearly forty years since their friendship came to an abrupt end, but I like to ask anyway because you never know when someone will have a change of heart. Apparently, nothing has changed because Oswald stiffened and said, 'Mr. Charles Pip would do well to stay in his office and me in mine.' You know those two used to be best friends with your dad, of course, and I think if he were alive, the two could get along. He was the Benjamin Rush to Oswald's Thomas Jefferson and Mr. Pip's John Adams. But, you know, I've planned to get those two in the same room again. They have both RSVP'd for my Easter brunch!"

Astrid nodded, "On that subject, do you have a specific décor in mind? Are we doing Easter-specific or general spring? Centerpieces? More importantly, how, pray tell, do you plan on getting Mr. Pip to your event, as he is not in the habit of socializing? He generally RSVPs in the affirmative and finds an ailment that necessitates his cancellation later."

"He stopped because he rather embarrassed himself years ago when he let his passions get away from him, insisting that no good comes from a lack of structure, expectations, and standards. He was going on about how failure is required for learning. Oswald argued that there is no need for expectations when manipulation is just as sufficient in providing the desired results; you don't need to hound people and chart progress when you can convince them to do what you want by appealing to their lazy natures. I was shocked to hear those words come out of Oswald's mouth. Are you not shocked?" Millie asked.

"Astonished, indeed! What was the starting topic, might I ask?" Astrid asked.

"You know I can't recall. I must have forgotten," Millie replied, looking over her shoulder three times before picking up a pen to fill out the order form.

"Have you now? I don't see you as a woman in the habit of forgetting an essential detail of what appears to be a pivotal conversation between two former friends," Roland chimed in.

"Hello, Roland. Your coaching career is coming along in a manner befitting a new coach. There are plenty of fumbles and foibles, wouldn't you agree?" Millie asked, her feathers ruffling.

Astrid saw Roland clench and unclench his fist, this time with his knuckles turning white, and intervened, "Millie, you were about to tell me how you will convince Mr. Pip to attend a social event? Does your technique involve bribery or blackmail?"

"Neither. I sent him a personalized invitation, mentioning that the allotment of school finances and extracurricular opportunities for children would be discussed. Plus, I am hosting the event at our old high school, which holds fond memories for him. Principles and duty predictably bind Mr. Pip. Nothing is dearer to his heart than children. He'll come," Millie said, proud of her genius.

"So, you lied to him?" Roland asked. "That's not very nice."

"It's not a lie, and I am nice. Charles well knows about my Easter brunch, and the consequences of the casual conversations held there. You will realize soon, Roland, that you can say the same thing in a thousand ways. The trick is to figure out how the person you are talking to will understand. He will not be able to cite his care of that red-headed child as a reason not to attend, as I also made an invitation addressed specifically to her, though I do not know her name. No matter, she is but a child, and my oversight likely went unnoticed," Millie said.

"How can you personalize an invitation if you do not know the name of the person you are addressing? What did you write, To the Red-Headed Child?" Roland asked. "A child is a person, and people have names. Her name is Nova."

"Let's review your order, shall we?" Astrid intervened once again. "Roses, peonies, hydrangeas, tulips, and lilies for the centerpiece on the main dining table, table accents with smaller versions of the same, three tall vases at the entryway filled with cherry blossoms, forsythia, and flowering branches, and a small posy tied with a powder-blue ribbon placed on each plate. Is there anything else you want me to add?"

"No, all is in order, though I simply must insist you attend as an active participant in the conversations, not a wallflower. And now that I think about it, adding a few Easter-specific decorations might add a touch of fun. All guests

are to bring a date, so invite someone handsome. Harold may be available. No one has seen him with any other women, and outside of his weekly visits here, not at all," Millie said.

"You know, whenever I come here and look at the pictures on the wall, I think of your Aunt Priscilla. As I am sure you know, she ran The Stealthy Picaroon for several years before she died. The woman was kind, thoughtful, and reserved, almost a doormat, truthfully, which likely contributed to her demise. When she went missing all those years ago, I prayed every day that she would be found. I think she is still out there."

Roland and Astrid exchanged confused glances, "What leads you to believe that she is still alive?"

Millie shook her head and wiped a tear from her eye. "I'm getting old and nostalgic, no other reason. It's more of a foolish hope. Your family and all of Doily Dayle lost more than we can imagine that day. But we shall not despair. On happier matters within our sphere, Stardust Silhouettes is having a sale on dresses if you are in want."

"I can say with confidence that Lottie is currently on a mission to pick through the sales rack meticulously," Astrid said as Millie took her hand in both of hers and gave it a gentle squeeze.

"If you find a dress you love, buy it no matter the cost. You never know how short life is—here today, gone tomorrow. Some pass far too young, others

live when all appearances suggest the impossibility of their next breath, and some of us try to bring little joys with parties and flowers. We'll see you soon. Have a lovely day," Millie said, stepping toward the door.

"Farewell, Millie," Roland offered with a forced smile.

"Roland," she replied with a nod and stiffening her shoulders. "I am enjoying driving my car without a broken window. That luxury aside, how much closer are you to creating the dream track meet for our youth?"

"The uniforms, shoes, bells, and whistles are, evidently, a vain and selfish cost, but with the help of a few reliable team members and friends, our youth will leave feeling important, which is my ultimate goal," Roland returned, forcing a pleasant smile.

Millie paused, the expression of snobbish needling giving way to compassion, "I'll be sure to bring the matter of funds to the forefront of Easter brunch conversations. As I said, many impactful decisions are discussed, and I did not realize you wanted to help our youth feel important. The scuttlebutt around town says that you are trying to create a public image for yourself and how ashamed your father would be of you if he could see how you are attempting to manipulate philanthropy for personal gain. Not to worry, I will set people straight."

Roland's gaze fell; every muscle in his body tightened, and unwelcome tears sprung to his eyes.

"Well, Millie, it's almost time for The Bloated Solution's $0.99 soda lunch special. We both know anyone can learn more about Doily Dayle during those two hours than reading a month of our city's periodicals," Astrid suggested as she came around the corner and walked her toward the door.

Giggling, Millie replied, "Indeed," before making her way down the sidewalk.

Astrid swiveled on her heel, elbows akimbo, an eyebrow raised as she looked at Roland. "Millie Rumorous would be an interesting choice as Adelaide's accomplice. She knows decades-worth of Doily Dayle gossip."

"You only have two decades, right?" Roland teased as he stood and hung an arm around Astrid's shoulder.

"She might have been a little tactless, but I think she is serious about helping to find funds for us."

"I am not amused, Roland, with you or her comment. But, I acknowledge that I know plenty of business that isn't mine. It's the capital with the highest return," Astrid said as she picked up her watering can to tend to the tulips. "Adelaide doesn't like people as a rule, so she would need someone competent in the information pedaling department to exact her revenge. Do you see what Millie did just now, trying to pull on my

heartstrings?"

"Maybe she meant everything she said," Roland offered. "I don't think she will ever forgive me for breaking her car window when I was nine. Little does she know that unfortunate incident was the beginning of my hockey career."

"She very well could have meant everything she said, but her sincerity does not exclude the possibility that she used it for diabolical purposes," Astrid said.

"Astrid, have you ever considered letting go of your vigilance for a week? Perhaps you should take a vacation. Where would you like to go? Ireland? France? Portugal? Thailand? The Netherlands? Yes, the Netherlands! They are known for their buttercup flowers, right? Did you not order your bulbs from there, if I recall correctly? What if I bought you and Lottie tickets? Would you go?"

"Not right now! I have a leaky water pipe to pay for, an Easter brunch to tend to, and I promised Nova that I would teach her how to dip marshmallows in chocolate," Astrid said.

"No truffles?" Roland asked.

"Not this time, maybe next."

"Darn it. I cannot change your mind or unburden you of your vigilance, but I can help you work on the wall. Dad taught me how to fix leaking water pipes. It's been a long while, but I'm sure we can

figure it out with a few reminders from the Internet," Roland said.

"What about your collarbone?" Astrid asked.

"I'll call Harold to come down, and we can do a switch-a-roo for the time being. I will be the brains, and he the brawn," Roland chuckled as he swiped his phone.

"If Harold has ever assisted with a plumbing job, consider me shocked," Astrid said.

"Dad taught him and me at the same time! Remember how Harold came along on all those car rides? Dad had a never-ending list of people who needed handyman work, and if the three of us were in the car, we were on our way to help someone," Roland explained.

"And consume ice cream cones, right? Mama did not tell me where you three went, but your faces bore the evidence," Astrid teased.

"Yes, soft-serve ice cream cones were part of our arrangement, and Mama was sworn to secrecy," Roland laughed. "She insisted that your schedule was full of books to read, stands to make, and people to talk with. You would have demanded on coming if you knew where we were going, and if you were refused, you would have exacted your revenge by burying tools or hiding Dad's list."

Astrid smiled and put her ear to the wall again. "She was right. I would have demanded and

shortly taken over the operation. Now, if you don't mind, please call Harold and ask him to come down here posthaste. Knowing I have a leaking water pipe makes me feel a bit like a fractious toddler."

"Sure, I'll give him a call. Would you mind running to get tools from Mama's garage? I'll text you a list. Don't worry, if your clients arrive, I shall direct any of their questions to your inbox," Roland said with a wink.

Harold answered and was on his way before Roland finished explaining the situation.

Harold and Frederick

When we last saw Harold, he had resigned from Moose University and cut ties with the socialite ecosystem that had sustained him. He maintained the legal and financial matters of the Braggart estate, though he found no satisfaction in what had become a necessary chore. Having never been under the illusion that he was surrounded by friends, for he had never been one himself, Harold had unwinding to do, unraveling, undoing. Who was he without the power he purchased from those who needed what only he could give them? Or, more accurately, the power he purchased from those who wanted what he claimed only he could give them. The exacting price of his choices was ever-present and ever-crushing.

Harold had no other recourse than a forthright conversation with the man looking back at him. No matter the cost of the glass or how intricate the frame is, a mirror is still a mirror and can no more hide the truth than a scale hides weight.

Dark hair, square chin, virile masculinity, and an expensive set of straight, bright teeth told of outward attractiveness, but his eyes were full of self-disgust, distrust, and discouragement. Questions such as, "What kind of a man am I? Why do I bother getting up in the morning?" plagued his mind. Thankfully, his hard-earned value of personal discipline kept him in his rigorous routine, the absence of which would have led to his inevitable demise. Awake early, a hard workout, work obligations, and keeping Frederick's healthcare on track kept him from the edge of internal destruction. Harold was grateful that Frederick required his attention and that his execution and communication skills could be used as tools rather than weapons.

Though he had let the staff of Braggart Mansion go with generous severance pay and reconciled all offenses and grievances that were within his power to reconcile, Harold vowed he would never forgive himself for his sins and became his own unyielding taskmaster.

The bright spot in Harold's life was, as it had ever been, Astrid Beeswax. When she walked out of his office on that horrible day at the hockey rink, he thought he had talked to her for the last time, that she hated him, and wished upon him the very cause of death that he had inadvertently afflicted upon her father. How the screams still sounded in his ears! The smell! Oh, that wretched smell.

However, when she left her forgiveness bouquet on one of the benches in the Braggart Garden, she also left a letter on scallop-edged stationery, complete with an embossed beehive seal, and signed with an A in bold, cursive hand.

Dear Harold, For years, I have imagined what I would say to you when the truth about my parents was made public, and they have lost all meaning to me now. I'm sorry for the personal tragedies you suffered. I never knew about your father and was too blinded by my rage to entertain the idea that Adelaide was as awful a mother as she is a person.

You suffered terribly, didn't you? You didn't deserve that. I don't know what living without unconditional love in every direction must be like. My life has been abundant with support. I don't say this to gloat or cut open a gangrenous wound with a dull and rusted knife but to offer compassion and extend mercy where none has been given.

You have been generous with your attention to me and my store since its inaugural opening. As penance for my contribution to your sorrows, you will find money to refund the dress I wore from Stardust Silhouettes at the masquerade ball. I probably owe you more than that, but this is what I can do for now.

Astrid

Harold had meticulously scrutinized Astrid's letter a dozen times, harboring a glimmer of hope that a word or phrase would wash away the ever-present sick pit in his stomach. Unfortunately, his diligence proved fruitless, yet he deemed that social rules required a response and replied to Astrid's correspondence with one of his own.

Realizing that candor would be uncomfortable for both of them, he ignored the impulse to write an unedited version of his experience as Adelaide's son. Instead, he crafted a handwritten reply, which languished within his desk drawer for days, subject to multiple revisions. The final draft was covered in eraser marks.

Dear Astrid,

Your words have touched me deeply and are a testament to your integrity and strength of character. You would be justified in slamming a gavel and pronouncing me condemned for my crimes against my fellow men, yet you offer compassion, mercy, and solace.

Furthermore, your gracious offer of penance is unnecessary, and I cannot accept payment for that which you did not purchase. Please use the funds toward your success and security.

I hope to become a better, good man. While in the process, I wonder if I might continue to pick up my weekly arrangement on Wednesdays at 2:00 PM?.

Harold

Astrid received his letter via post and wrote back,

Dear Harold,

Your order will be honored as before, and discussions on gardening and botany are readily available at your request.

Astrid

When Harold reappeared, he seemed stripped of his elite ideals and arrogance; even his posture had changed. His chin was at an average level rather than tilted upward, and his smile was not as quick to come. Aside from the public humiliation and career annihilation he had experienced, the acute burden came from the slow realization of the enormity of taking responsibility for his father's care.

With Adelaide's absence no longer casting an unpredictable shadow over the Braggart Mansion like a tempestuous cloud, Harold arranged for Frederick to move into the 7,000-square-foot abode.

Each of its seven bedrooms boasted lavish comforts: sumptuous carpets, fine linen, and antique furnishings, complemented by individual bathrooms featuring claw-foot tubs, marble countertops, and ornate fixtures. In Frederick's younger years, he had curated his sanctuary: a meticulously designed library with books spanning a myriad of disciplines —chemistry, robotics, anatomy, physiology, marine biology, and an array of other natural sciences. Vintage volumes, including prized first editions, adorned one wall, while other celebrated modern works spanning architecture, art, philosophy, and fiction. The room of endless learning had been vacant for years, only entered to be dusted.

Adding to the uniqueness of the austere mansion was a recently transformed kitchen. Since there were two, Harold turned the smaller one into a personal bean-to-bar chocolate production room, equipped with the tools of the trade: a roaster, winnower, melangeur, conch, molds of various shapes and sizes, and other odds and ends necessary for the generation of chocolates. Harold needed something to hyper-focus on that did not require emotional investment. After so many hours searching for a worthy challenge, single-sourced, small-batch chocolate won his favor.

When considering how to create comfortable and tailored accommodations for Frederick, Harold reflected on the countless times he had observed his father engrossed in scientific endeavors, meticulously jotting down equations and experimental results.

He often regretted the absence of his father's preserved papers, thinking they held clues to the past.

Nonetheless, he devised an alternative plan: reinstating Frederick in his library, equipping him with a freshly sharpened number two pencil, and providing a sheet of college-ruled paper on the table. Perhaps, Harold hoped, if Frederick were treated like a human being, with respect and consideration for his genius despite the outward struggle, he might find some degree of healing that medication could never offer.

Upon reviewing the chart notes discreetly tucked away in a drawer within Frederick's garden cottage, Harold swiftly prioritized the need for a qualified psychiatric care physician. The original doctor, handpicked by Adelaide, operated under a cash-only arrangement to circumvent the complexities of insurance procedures and audits. Given Adelaide's self-serving nature, Harold harbored reservations about entrusting Frederick's care to this doctor. Instead, he sought out Dr. Ebenezer Sereneheart, recognizing his promising expertise based on readings from medical journals and peer-reviewed research.

Hailing from London, Dr. Sereneheart possessed a distinctive English accent, warm amber-brown eyes, a mass of unruly curls atop his head, and a broad smile that immediately put others at ease. His athletic physique, upright posture, and large hands conveyed gentle confidence, compassion, and empathy.

A constant state of nervousness marked Frederick's demeanor, his unease palpable in every interaction. In contrast, Dr. Sereneheart patiently approached Frederick's condition, calmly guiding him through each appointment with gentle reassurance. Despite Harold's fervent hope for his father's mental health to be restored to its former strength, he soon confronted the harsh reality of Frederick's unpredictable behavior. One moment, Frederick would be diligently working at his desk or tending to the garden, only to vanish the next. Desperate for answers, Harold scoured the estate in frantic searches, only to walk inside and find Frederick resuming his activities as if nothing had happened, his countenance unchanged—distant and wholly absorbed in his tasks.

Faced with Frederick's baffling disappearances and the lack of clarity from security footage, Harold found solace in the idea of transforming Frederick's cottage into a dedicated patient room under Dr. Sereneheart's guidance. Dr. Sereneheart, recognizing the limitations of Frederick's current medication regimen, echoed Harold's sentiments, suggesting that the prescribed medications seemed counterproductive, potentially exacerbating Frederick's cognitive condition rather than alleviating it. Harold's initial impulse to pursue legal action against Frederick's previous doctor was fueled by frustration and indignation. However, his attempts to locate her in online provider databases yielded no results.

"Adelaide wins again," he had muttered under his breath as he closed his laptop, silently wondering why she would go to such extraordinary lengths to avoid any medical intervention that might help.

The pain of witnessing Frederick's daily struggle weighed heavily on Harold's heart, and he determinedly scoured every nook and cranny of the mansion for evidence of secrets. Adelaide was full of them; why would the mansion be any different? Surprisingly, he stumbled upon an old shoebox tucked away in a forgotten corner while remodeling the kitchen into his personal chocolate factory—a relic of what was once Adelaide's heart, it seemed.

With trembling hands, he pried open the box to find pictures of his childhood before Ingrid had died, and Frederick lost his mind: Ingrid and Harold fingerpainting. Ingrid and Harold having a water balloon fight in the backyard. Ingrid and Harold taking a nap on the couch, their chubby sun-kissed cheeks covered in sticky melted ice cream, their hair tangled from dirt and sunscreen. Ingrid and Frederick carrying a robin-blue wicker Easter basket filled with candy. Ingrid on Frederick's shoulders, laughing and hugging his head. Harold and Frederick sitting at the kitchen table, solving a math problem. Through the photographs, Harold recognized a characteristic he knew they shared: an intensity that would repel or attract whoever or whatever was necessary.

When the emotional devastation of realization dropped upon him in its entirety, a sob forced its way out of Harold's heart before he clamped his hand over his mouth. Working on math problems at the kitchen table was one of his few happy memories; his dad looked as solid and capable as he remembered. Sometimes, as kids, heroes seem prettier, stronger, taller, smarter, and more impressive than they are.

Parents and caretakers can be imagined as invincible, omniscient, and omnipotent. Invariably, they fall off the magically made pedestal and are seen as mortals with gifts, shortcomings, successes, and failures. But, when an accident or illness befalls the hero before their mortality is known, they become forever engrained in the mind as the one who could do no wrong. So, Harold clung to the belief that one man's physical, mental, and emotional presence could have prevented so much. And that belief became his fuel.

As Harold continued to examine the photo of him and his father at the kitchen table, he thought that surely seeing such a touching memory would ignite activity in Frederick's amygdala, the part of the brain where emotional memories are encoded and stored. And, if the amygdala could be ignited, could the prefrontal cortex, temporal lobe, and cerebellum not be ignited as well? Even the whole brain?

Knowing he was no neuroscientist, Harold tested his hope anyway. He chose a moment when Frederick was contentedly working amidst his rose bushes in Braggart Gardens.

"Dad? Dad, it's me, Harold," he stammered as he slowly approached his dad and handed him the photograph.

Frederick laid down his spade, his weathered hands taking Harold's proffered gift and holding it gently. He smoothed the edges and held it closer to his eyes before murmuring, "My boy."

"Yes, Dad, yes, your boy. That boy is me. I'm your boy. I'm Harold!" Harold pleaded in desperation, his hopes rising exponentially with each second. He repeatedly pointed between the picture and himself as he felt the chasm of lost time and fractured memories widening.

As Frederick's gaze met Harold's, it bore the

burden of sorrow too heavy to bear, knowing someone important stood before him while knowing he couldn't remember who or why. For all that he did not know and could not remember, Frederick knew that he had once been part of the vibrant world that shut him away.

"Do you know me, Dad?" Harold implored once more.

Frederick shook his head once and uttered with profound loss, "My boy," before handing the picture back to Harold.

Harold felt as if his hope had been irreparably destroyed like a landslide during a typhoon. But then, as Frederick picked up his spade, he whispered, "I love my boy."

Tears streamed uncontrollably down Harold's face, first for the words his dad spoke and second for the realization that he could not remember hearing anyone tell him that they loved him. Had he ever said those words to anyone else? Had he felt love for anyone besides himself? And really, he admitted, he didn't love himself; he loved getting attention, having the answers, and being in control.

Yes, he talked with Astrid and Roland, but he felt undeserving of their kindness and had thrown away any chance of becoming interwoven bosom friends. Harold saw himself as a monster, a selfish brute. By any outside measurement, a selfish brute is precisely what he had been.

But transformation is a beautiful gift; he needn't stay as he was. Simply hearing Frederick say, "I love my boy," broke a chip off Harold's shoulder.

Ideals of combatting selfishness are easily entertained when alone but difficult in practice, though made easier for the desire. Since there is no better place to practice selflessness than at home, Harold began every morning by asking Frederick, "How can I help you?" His response included handing Harold the tool needed for the day's work.

On a rainy Monday, Frederick directed Harold toward the dimly lit kitchen. He handed him a number two pencil, lined paper, and a book titled *Making Chocolate,* which Harold had recently purchased. For himself, Frederick had sheets of paper already filled with algorithms and curious renderings of engineered spectacles. Unable to determine what the documents meant and refusing the idea that Frederick's work was invariably void of cohesive intelligence, he snapped a picture with his phone while his dad was in the bathroom. When Frederick returned, he looked from his papers to Harold and back again, sat down, put his arm around his work as if hiding the answers on a test from a cheating classmate, and said, "None of your business. None of your business. Hidden.

Priscilla. Stolen. Lost."

Love Prepared for the Heartache

"Astrid!" Nova proclaimed on the other side of the shared picket fence as Astrid pulled into her driveway and stepped out of her car, "I am learning Portuguese, and did you know that in Portuguese, the word for potato is *patata*? I can yell louder than anyone at school. See?" Nova paused to gather all available air in her ambitious lungs. "Patata! Patata! Patata! Patata! Patata! Patata!" Nova's smile covered her entire face.

"And over there in the grass is Jasper. He is lying down right now because he's having a sleeping attack. He's the boy I told you about who was mean to my daughters. We had a chat, just like you said, and I think he's a real swell kind of kid. He likes birds, especially chickens. I asked Mr. Pip if I could get chickens, and he said he would think about it, which is his way of saying no, basically."

"Ba-cluck! Ba-cluck!" suddenly, a nearly translucent boy with stick-like appendages, blonde

hair fashioned in a buzz cut, and braces jumped up with his arms mimicking chicken wings. "Ba-cluck!" He scratched at the ground with his feet as he followed Nova around the fence.

"Hello, Jasper. I am pleased to make your acquaintance," Astrid said as she held her hand to shake his. The nearly translucent boy got closer to her, bobbing and tilting his head. He looked up through round, steel blue eyes before screaming, "Ba-cluck!" and pecking her palm.

"Let me see if I have some chicken feed," Astrid laughed. With her other hand, she grabbed a handful of gummy bears from her purse and held them out for his eager consumption. He ate them one at a time, which is as fast as chicken pecking allows.

"Gummy bears! This is the best day of my life! Patata! Patata! Patata!" Nova yelled, snatching the rest of the gummy bears before lifting her neon green butterfly catcher high and running in the opposite direction.

"Ba-cluck! Ba-cluck!" yelled Jasper, chasing after her with short, quick steps and wildly flapping arms.

The Fire Child's untamed red tresses sparkled like fireworks in the sun. "Hey Jasper, let's have a screaming contest!"

"Please consider a sunscreen contest instead! You do not want to get a sunburn and suffer from the

terrible itching that follows or the long-term consequences of sun damage," Astrid yelled out while waving spray-on sunscreen above her head.

Alas, she spoke too late. The screaming contest was underway before she said her last syllable, and the margin between the winner and loser was narrow indeed.

"What are those horrid noises?" Beatrice Beeswax asked as her daughter walked through the front door and into the kitchen.

"What you are hearing is a patata and a chicken having a screaming contest," Astrid explained, trying to massage the pain out of her ears.

"Nova told you about her Portuguese lessons, too?" Beatrice asked.

"Yes, and now she has a friend to scream with, so I am sure her life has become exponentially more super duper a million times exciting, if that's even possible," Astrid sighed while tearing a pale pink napkin into tiny pieces. "I hope her parents get to watch her from heaven occasionally."

Beatrice nodded in agreement. "I don't know what saddens me more: Nova growing up without her parents or her parents watching from a distance that cannot be traversed in this life. Not being able to hold your child, kiss their head, give them hugs, make their favorite dessert, praise their effort, measure their growth spurts, listen to their life, soothe their cries, and teach them how to thread a needle would be enough to break a parent's heart."

"Thread a needle?" Astrid asked.

"If only I had caught that on video. You were so furious when Roland learned quicker than you that you lectured your father on the absurdity of the lesson," Beatrice said with a wistful smile. "I can guarantee that your father weeps for all he cannot touch and cannot do, but he is so proud of who you have become. I remember his excitement when he learned you inherited his radio antenna ears. Do you want to watch the recording with me?"

"I don't know if he is proud of me, but yes, I want to watch the recording! What recording are we talking about? How long is the video?" Astrid asked, glancing at the numerical clock on the wall.

"Why are you in a hurry?" Beatrice asked.

"There is a leaking pipe in the wall at The Bee's Knees, and Harold and Roland are diagnosing the problem.

Roland gave me a list of tools to retrieve from the garage. However, they can wait, as can my clients. Some days, I want to sleep in, overeat, and slip into a delicious depression, marinating in can nots and have nots until doubt and despair have returned as familiar companions," Astrid said, wiping a tear from her eye.

"Oh, Astrid. If only you could give yourself grace and time. To answer your question, the video is

only a few minutes," Beatrice answered.

"Self-grace is self-excuse, and you know how I loathe excuses from others. I shall not tolerate a speck of excuse in myself. Should we wait to watch it with Roland? I don't want him to feel sad if he realizes I saw it before him," Astrid said.

Beatrice took Astrid's hand and squeezed it tight. "Roland has never and will never be in competition with you. He will want to spend time alone with the memory, too. Come, let us watch. Do you want to tell me what tripped the wire and let loneliness and unrealistic expectations block your path?"

Generally, when she spoke with her mother, Astrid was either a drought or a mudslide of personal feelings.

On days when holding the mudslide back felt like a Herculean task, she often thought she should carry a sign that said, "Danger: Mudslide Season," so that any individual brave enough to engage in conversation with her could prepare themselves with proper safety equipment.

With her emotional capital already used up, the mudslide was inevitable. "Why do I treat emotions like they are living souls with more control over my brain than me? Does loneliness have a heartbeat? A cognitive brain? A need for food, air, and water? Loneliness only lives if it feeds on my emotions— like a leech that insists on telling me that if I am drained of blood, I will have more power. Shall I be forever in pursuit of Accomplishment that never ceases to evade me no matter how hard I work? Am I so concerned with my appearance that I give no thought to the resources I waste on myself that could be given to those without any clothes at all? Oh, Mama, I have never fit in. How can I be too much and not enough all at once? Too loud, too opinionated, too what? Does the presence of someone with purpose and passion make others squirm? Must women cut each other at the base and tear off wings piece by piece, one at a time? I tried to participate in the conversation, but my face talked too loudly. I tried to care about what they cared about, but I simply didn't."

"Did one of your old schoolmates come to place an order recently?" Beatrice asked.

Astrid, already fully launched into her diatribe against herself, could not hear her mother. "I can tell a story that entertains, but the connection isn't there when one heart speaks to another, even if their words are wildly insufficient. Crowds and groups are exhausting because a collective human energy pings around instead of moving forward.

Is the weather all that interesting? Are political affiliations the shields we hide behind, fighting over what we cannot change instead of getting to know one another? What keeps people up at night? What makes people laugh so hard that they cry? Maybe I need to ask better questions. Or wear my pajamas and call it casual athletic wear. Yes, I shall don my jammies, put my hair in an uncombed knot atop my head, forgo shaping undergarments in the name of being liberated, end every sentence with, 'you know what I'm saying,' forgetting the 'do' entirely, and complain about the facets of my life in which I have complete control as if I am nothing more than an amorphous blob hoping to be swept up by the wind of luck and placed majestically on the ground of Perfect Things."

Beatrice tried not to laugh or smile. She did not think her daughter's words funny; she found joy in Astrid's doing one of the many things that made her Astrid. She said, "I advise against leading with those sentiments, though you and Roland seem to struggle similarly. Perhaps, and this is merely a suggestion, you might try finding those with whom you belong instead of thinking that the only way to make new friends is to fit in. Besides, you don't want to fit in anyway."

"I have already found the people with whom I belong, but two of them have been largely unavailable for months. Besides, Mama, all blessings come with curses. Remember how Dad needed a long rest after one of your social engagements? He would come home and nap for one, two, or even three hours, completely worn out.

I wanted him to get up and play with me, and when he didn't, I would get so sad."

"I know you would," Beatrice said, knowing the less said, the better.

"And pray, do not mistake my intentions, for I harbor no doubt regarding Dad's affection—a love so steadfast he sacrificed every comfort to provide mine. Nor do I seek to cast aspersions upon his fondness nor chide his penchant for repose. I am acquainted with the sensation of expending every ounce of my soul's vitality to stifle the urge to unleash a primal scream amidst an overwhelming clamor. Each squeak of a worn tennis shoe, the discordant clang of pots and dishes, the rumble of passing cars, the incessant click-clack of fingers upon a keyboard or thumbs on a phone, and the reverberation of voices, robust and resonant, assail my senses with unyielding ferocity. To fixate upon a solitary conversation amidst this tumult is a feat beyond the reach of mortal faculties. Frequently, I find myself teetering upon the precipice of hysteria, as though the very strands of my being are rent asunder. Thus, I have fashioned a refuge amidst the walls and organization of The Bee's Knees, a semblance of solitude amidst the noise, where I may find respite from the relentless onslaught of sounds. I also seek out sounds so you can see our tumultuous relationship. I know what I shall do! I shall bake biscotti," Astrid said, wiping away tears as she opened the wrong cupboards.

"Come now, Astrid. Per your words, you do not have the time to make biscotti, and you must look at yourself through a different lens. Thankfully, Roland was over here the other day, helping me go through old boxes. We found a few VHS tapes, and he asked Lottie to transfer the content to a digital format, which she did in no time. As is her way, she

did more than was asked and has made it immediately accessible.

Now, all I need to do is command Alexa to play *Beeswax Family Memories*. Come, watch your father, and feel his love wash over you and wash away these destructive thoughts," Beatrice said as she led the way to the living room.

"I have time to make the dough," Astrid began.

"No, you do not. Sit down. Alexa, play *Beeswax Family Memories*," Beatrice said firmly as the video began.

***

In the backyard of the Beeswax residence, when a wooden play structure still stood with its metal slide and a yellow plastic bucket swing, and the grass was littered with balls, shovels, babydolls, crayons, cups, and popsicle sticks, Aloysius sat cross-legged with a banjo, strumming a tune. Before him were two cherubic three-year-olds, their innocent emerald green eyes gleaming with curiosity and mischief. Roland's black, curly hair was unruly, his face covered in mud or chocolate, possibly both, and he was donning blue coveralls.

Sitting patiently, he glances admiringly at his dad between examining blades of grass, elusive praying mantises, the finger that had been inside of his nose, and giggling. Astrid's head tilted to one side or another, following the sounds of birds. She leaned her ear to the grass and squealed, "Red

bug!" before the insect crawled into her field of vision. Her toddler mind jumped to the next sounds and the next as if she wanted to pay attention to all of them but had no choice but to give a quick 'hello' before moving on. Before long, little Astrid covered her ears and started crying.

"What is making my sweet girl so sad?" Aloysius asked, scooping her in his long arms and holding her close to his chest.

"Outside too loud!" she cried, kicking her legs and scrunching her face.

Aloysius hugged her tight before wiping away her tears, and standing her shiny Mary Jane-clad feet on his legs,

"What do you hear?" he asked.

Astrid pointed at Mr. Pip's fence and whispered, "Dog."

"Yes, Fezziwig, the border collie even breathes loud, doesn't he?"

Astrid nodded.

"What else do you hear?" Aloysius asked.

"Kitty cats. Bumblebees. Cars," Astrid whispered again

"I can hear them, too. That's a lot of sounds all at once, isn't it?"

Astrid's tiny black brows furrowed into a deep frown, and her lower lip made for a comical scowl as she slowly nodded her head.

Aloysius hugged her again, "Astrid Beeswax, listen carefully because I am about to tell you something very important. Are you ready?" She nodded and buried her face on his shoulder.

"I want to see your beautiful eyes when I tell you this," he said, gently bringing her face back before his. "You have been given an extraordinary gift, the same gift that my mother gave to me. Can you point to your ears?"

Little Astrid immediately pointed to her ears. "You're right! Those are your ears, and your ears can hear more than other ears can. Sometimes, you will feel like you do right now, overwhelmed and maybe a little scared. I did, too, and there are days when I still do. That's okay.

"As you grow up, if you learn to listen beyond the sounds, you will hear when someone needs to feel loved. Maybe the person will be your mama or brother, or maybe it will be a stranger, but when you hear that sound, you can help. You must learn the sound for yourself, which may be incredibly frustrating. But remember, you are full of the light and love this world needs. Others may not understand, and they don't need to. Never stop listening because others cannot hear what you can."

"Aloysius, she is three," Beatrice said in the background. "Don't overwhelm her."

Aloysius looked toward the camera, winked, and then kissed his cherub on the forehead, "You're recording this, right? She might not understand what I am saying right now, but she will need to hear it in the future, and I might not always be around."

"You have plans to live as a mentally and physically vigorous young man until you are 112. I think you will be around to tell her," Beatrice replied.

Aloysius shrugged before setting Astrid on the grass and picking up Roland.

***

"We'll skip over this next part," Beatrice said. "Roland should be the first to see the wisdom his father has for him. However, we can watch my favorite part."

***

"Let's sing our favorite song!" Aloysius suggested as he raised his long arms to conduct his toddler choir. Astrid stood up to dance accordingly while Roland dug deeper into the dirt, scolding it for containing pebbles. She sang a few words but was immediately distracted again by the sound of kitten footsteps.

"I hear kitty!" she exclaimed.

Aloysius paused and asked, "Where is the kitty?"

"Kitchen!" Astrid said as she pumped her chubby legs toward the sliding glass door, Roland in pursuit, clenching a fistful of dirt over his head as if he had stolen buried treasure and the rightful owner was in pursuit.

"That poor kitty. I'll save him from his assailants," Aloysius said as he stood up, caught the twins in his arms, put one on either shoulder, and ran a few circles around the yard. He stopped breathlessly before the camera with a goofy smile on his face.

"I lub my dad," little Astrid and Roland said in unison before squishing their squishy cheeks against his.

"Do I have mud and chocolate on my face now?" Aloysius asked his wife.

"Chocolate, mud, and maybe some popsicle juice," Beatrice answered. "All three of you best wash your face before you come closer to me. As you can see, I am wearing my new white cardigan."

"Come on over here, Beatrice. White cardigans can be replaced. The camera can stand on its own," Aloysius said. Beatrice stood on her tiptoes and kissed the cheeks of all three before Aloysius leaned down and gave her a big kiss on the lips. The cherubs squealed some more, and the happiest moment in a humble backyard on a sunny day was captured for the rest of the time.

***

Silent tears streamed down Astrid's face. "How did Dad know I would need to hear his words in the future? Do you think he had a feeling he was going to pass away at a fairly young age?"

"I have learned not to plague myself with such thoughts. They only serve to darken my happy memories, which are too valuable to tarnish. Be content with knowing that your father loved you with all his heart," Beatrice said, retaking Astrid's hand. "And find peace knowing I love you and have been your cheerleader in every chapter of your life.

"Do you want to see one more scene and we can save the rest for later? This will only take thirty seconds; it's you repeating your favorite line from your one-girl production of *A Christmas Carol*. Although, before I show it to you, you must oblige to a reboot this coming Christmas."

"Very well. I accept your conditions," Astrid said.

Sure enough, at Beatrice's command, Astrid soon heard her adolescent voice repeating, "Business! Mankind was my business. The common welfare was my business; charity, mercy, forbearance, and benevolence, were, all, my business. The dealings of my trade were but a drop of water in the comprehensive ocean of my business!"

***

After the home video ended, Astrid felt inoculated

with love against all the lies that would tear her down. With a confident step and squared shoulders, she walked to her car.

"Hiya, Astrid! It's me, Nova! Some woman walked by and told me to give you this," Nova said, handing her a vintage brown envelope sealed with a yellow Beeswax seal. "Birdie Blankie says that I should not eat candy that strangers give me, and I don't think you should read letters that strangers give you. Is it awkward if a dog marries a human?"

"Very. Thank you Nova, both for the letter and the advice," Astrid said, throwing the letter onto the passenger seat. Driving the short distance between home and work, she vacillated between keeping and disposing of the letter, weighing the pros and cons. Unsurprisingly, curiosity won.

To My Darling Astrid,

The impossibility of this letter strikes me as much as it does you, yet here we both are. Like father like daughter, we shall imagine each other's joy as we imagine the writer and the reader anticipating what comes next.

When you were young, you often came home with one of your white ruffled socks tattered; your hat stepped on, or a grass stain on your dress. Given your preference for beauty and order, I thought you would be infuriated by whatever led to your disheveled state. But I was wrong. Your frustration was aimed at whatever perceived unfairness you witnessed, and I was proud that you desired to live in a world where all people regarded all others as their equals.

Unfortunately, from where I sit, you have become a beautiful and stunning woman who thinks she is better than those around her. Your outfits are magnificent, and if your mother could see them, she would agree, but you look like a little girl playing dress up or a middle schooler trying to find herself. Your personality and opinions occupy too much space; must you selfishly demand more attention by reminding those around you of how little they have?

Your Affectionately Disappointed Father,

Aloysius Beeswax

*If you learn to listen beyond the sounds, you will
hear when someone needs to feel loved.*

Regarding Priscilla

Harold arrived at The Bee's Knees within minutes of Astrid's departure. He almost startled himself when he saw his reflection in the casement window. His haircut was the same as before, a finger-combed pompadour with a clean fade, though he no longer cared how it fell. Expensive suits, belts, cufflinks, shoes, and ties remained in his closet in exchange for denim jeans, t-shirts, flannel jackets, and sweaters, depending on the weather. All well-fitted and of the highest quality.

More noticeable than the wardrobe was the lack of electronic engagement. He had one phone, which he primarily kept on silent, one watch, which was only a watch, and a pair of ten-dollar sun spectacles. True, every so often, the thought of returning to the public eye flitted across his mind. All he would need to do was don his fancy duds, make a few calls, procure a flashy car, call in favors, maybe throw a few parties, and take selfies with socially prominent individuals, specifically the pretty ones.

However, there was no longer fertile ground for that seed of thought to take root. Frederick needed him, making the idea of keeping a foot in both worlds absurd.

When he saw Astrid's car was gone, a brief disappointment danced across his face, but seeing Millie Rumorous in an animated conversation with an innocent passerby reminded him of their recent shared amusement.

***

After Adelaide's disappearance, Millie took no time in telling anyone who would listen that she had witnessed Harold walking into The Bee's Knees once a week for years. For a few weeks, she had made a nuisance of herself by entering the floral shop behind Harold. Astrid, annoyed, told Harold that she recalled overhearing Millie at a party where she disclosed to Adelaide that she was plagued with the fear that somewhere, somehow, a duck was watching her. Adelaide responded in her predictably calloused way, "If you want to remain my friend, I beg you never to mention your insanity again. I cannot abide quirks in anyone. Every new best friend must be exactly like the one before."

So, to address Millie's unwelcome presence, Astrid, at great amusement to Harold, pretended to have a tantalizing piece of gossip, beckoned Millie to the counter, leaned forward, and whispered, "Don't tell anybody because this is a rather peculiar acquisition of information, but I heard from another client that the duck population is expected to increase by 382% in the next three years. How will our community accommodate so many? If you do not think that statistic is bizarre, there is more to the story. My client said he swears he saw a mallard watching him through his window. I told him he did not need to worry because ducks have panoramic vision and less acuity than humans. However, he then told me that ducks have a third eyelid called the nictitating membrane that protects their eyes while submerged in water. Think of the possibilities, Millie! The ducks could be watching us right now!"

"Who did you say this client was?" Millie asked as her face went bleak and colorless.

"I did not mention a name, only that I was told. You look quite ill, Millie. Do you need to sit down, or can I get you something to drink? Water? Lemonade?" Astrid asked.

"No, no," Millie politely declined, covering her mouth with a napkin. "I must have eaten some disagreeable food for lunch. If you will excuse me, I will come back another time."

"I do hope you feel better. A fizzy drink from The Bloated Solution might help," Astrid called after her.

"Oh, dear. I think she might vomit. Now, I feel bad."

Harold stifled a laugh, "I have never heard Millie say she was leaving voluntarily. When she visited my mother, Adelaide would threaten to call security before she would finally leave."

"How often did she visit your mother?" Astrid asked.

"Often enough that she was a regular fixture in our house," Harold replied.

"I am sure she kept the room bright."

***

The recent memory chased away Harold's disappointment, and he joined Roland in assessing the leaking water pipe.

"Hello, Harold. Thank you for coming down on such short notice, and please do not inquire about my collarbone injury. I went mountain biking and went off a jump. My shoes were unclipped, the handlebars went awry, and I landed shoulder first, like a lawn dart in the dirt. I'll be better soon enough. Now, as far as I can tell, the leak is localized and will require minimally invasive surgery, so to speak. I sent Astrid home to get the tools," Roland explained.

"Why did you do that? I have a bucket full of tools right here," Harold said, holding up a five-gallon bucket filled with screwdrivers, pliers, an adjustable wrench, a hammer, measuring tape, a level, Allen wrenches of various sizes, and work

gloves.

"I suppose we can consider ourselves the beneficiaries of double coverage. Thank you so much for coming, Harold," Astrid said as she walked in with another five-gallon bucket and a tear-stained face. "I grabbed everything on the list and a few snacks: lemon biscotti, raspberries, popcorn, and chocolate."

"Why were you crying?" Harold asked, with furrowed brows and a creased forehead.

 "I thought Lottie was coming back with fizzy drinks and cookies," Roland said, knowing how embarrassed Astrid got if anyone saw her cry. "She is, but I guarantee she shops every sales rack within a four-mile radius. Two hours have already passed," Astrid said. "Harold, thank you for your concern, but I suffer only from the stories I tell myself. Now, if I could learn to stop reading the stories, I would find myself tear free."

"Huh, you're probably right on both counts," Roland said, using the 'probably' to permit himself to silently disagree with her without telling a lie.

"I am 100% correct," Astrid insisted.

"It's okay to cry," Harold said, taking a rose from a vase, handing it to her, and grimacing at his awkwardness.

Astrid took the rose, brought it to her nose, blushed, spun on her heel, and walked toward the

cash register. Harold smiled and began looking for the screwdriver already in plain sight, and Roland extended Astrid the kindness of pretending not to notice.

Ever the protective brother and a man of simplicity, he had never found cause to defend Astrid as she possessed a strength and resilience that often left little need for external intervention. Nor did he harbor any inclination to dictate the actions of others. Yet, at that moment, he began to doubt whether the changes in Harold were permanent, and to wonder what the ramifications would be if his doubts proved correct. He might have ignored his concern on another day and at another time.

Leaning toward Harold, he whispered, "Hey, we both know how you feel about her, so I will say this once and leave the rest between you and Astrid. If you take advantage of her through mental or emotional manipulation or cause harm to come upon her through your selfishness, I'm going to have a problem, which means you will have a problem. Understood?" Roland asked, his eyes more intensely focused and his voice sharper than Harold had ever heard.

The two men locked eyes as they had many times on the ice, only this time Harold humbly submitted, "Understood."

Astrid, who insisted that The Bee's Knees phone be kept on a coiled cord, was twirling in it as she

spoke to the client on the other end. She caught Harold's eye and smiled. He turned to Roland and reiterated, "I will never hurt your sister."

"Good," was Roland's terse response. A few uncomfortable moments passed before he continued,

"Shall we get started on the wall?"

"We shall," Harold said. "Are you and Lottie going to attend Millie's Easter brunch?"

"Lottie plans on going. I will not be going because I do not want to. Furthermore, I don't care for brunches, dressing up, talking about matters that no one is willing to take action on, and fretting over which utensil to use," Roland said.

Harold nodded, "You see, people think they are doing something when they are arguing over something of which their opinions will never change, with someone who will never agree with them. If one wants more control, one only needs to fuel the fight. Bloodthirsty contention will do its own work in due course. Rules of the game aside, are you doing alright? You don't sound like your usual cheerful self, concern for Astrid notwithstanding."

Roland pointed to his shoulder. "I will be much better when I can move around again. I've been so irritable that even Lottie needed a break. But, enough about me. Back to the leaking water pipe. It's something we can fix. If I can't fix an issue, I would truly prefer not to know about it."

"You would live a lonely life full of unrealistic expectations if you only knew about the problems you could fix. Your company would include only yourself. To truly know anyone is to know their struggles and imperfections; otherwise, you know only what your eyes tell you—" Astrid began as she rejoined the men.

"Or your ears," Roland interrupted.

"Yes, any of your five senses," Astrid said. "You must observe with your heart. My roommate was at least one hundred pounds overweight during college. When we first met, I judged her, thinking that she had brought upon herself her health problems and that the weight was simply a matter of a lack of self-discipline. Then, we ended up in the same chemistry class and worked on the same project. As I got to know her, I learned that she had suffered through the death of her parents, had sustained many injuries, suffered from depression, endured physical restraints that prevented her from participating in many activities and was all around full of sadness without any perceivable recourse. The more she spoke, the more compassion I had for her because it was easy to see myself in her place. There is not as wide as a chasm between those who suffer from any number of addictions and those who don't."

"'An accident, an illness, or three poor choices,' as Dad used to say," Roland added.

"Are you still friends?" Harold asked.

"No, not really. I have not seen or heard from her in years. Sorry for the abrupt change in topic, but I must confess that my brain is in dire need of a challenge of a unique sort. A problem to solve, a mystery to uncover, or a new talent to learn."

"What you need is a project!" Roland declared. "I cannot believe I forgot what I brought in my pocket, but Millie reminded me. I was ruminating over her rudeness when I remembered."

"Do you have a project in your pocket?" Astrid asked.

"Indeed, I do," Roland said as he pulled an old picture from his wallet. "And, a mystery. In her merciful pity—I mean compassion—Mama asked me to help her go through old boxes with pictures and trinkets. She's been looking for the original copy of her first published children's book, *The Giraffe's Resistance*, and can't recall where she last put it, though she assures me that it was in a safe and special location. I don't think she cares about the book nearly so much as she was trying to find a way to lift my spirits."

"I hope this doesn't sound rude, but how does your mom look for things if she is blind?" Harold asked.

"She looks with her fingers," Astrid explained. "Her palpation skills are par excellence. Mama has always excelled at putting things in safe places and never finding them again," Astrid laughed, then

turned back to Roland. "Did you find the book?"

"Not yet, but hope remains because there are still more boxes. Alternatively, she may have it neatly tucked away in her drawer and is only using the feigned lost book as a ruse," Roland said.

"Are you going to tell me who is in that picture or continue covering the face with your thumb?" Astrid asked, craning her neck to get a better look.

Roland gave a mischievous smile as he handed Astrid the black-and-white photograph. "I have a mystery for you to solve and one to help you sharpen your detective skills. This is a picture of our Aunt Priscilla. Millie was right. You and she look nearly identical, right down to the affinity for dresses. Her nose is a bit wider than yours, or at least Mama said that is what she thought the one time she saw the picture of Priscilla."

"What detective skills are you talking about?" Harold asked.

"Aside from her picture on the wall, I remember Dad mentioning her once after I put together my first dress ensemble. I am surprised he didn't talk about her more often," Astrid mused, ignoring Harold's question and tracing Priscilla's attire with her graceful pointer finger.

"I said the same thing to Mama, who said that some pain has no words. But, you have ears and eyes, so, I propose you solve the missing person case of Priscilla Beeswax. You might uncover many

secrets in the process," Roland said, the thunderbolts from earlier giving way to a happy twinkle.

"A missing person case that is at least forty years old? What do we know about her? Did Mama give you any additional information, other than what Dad told us years ago?" Astrid asked, retrieving her trusty purple pen and paper.

"Mama has no more information than we do. Priscilla went missing at age twenty-eight; before that, she ran The Stealthy Picaroon by herself for several years. Grammy and Grandpa closed down the chocolate shop when the search ceased," Roland said.

Astrid scrutinized the image once more, "Roland, do you recognize the man with his arm around her?"

Roland leaned forward, "I admit that I did not pay much attention once I realized he was not Dad. But he does seem familiar, doesn't he? Any idea who he is?"

Astrid smile widened as she adjusted her hat, "This man is Frederick Braggart, a relatively young Frederick Braggart. Harold can confirm. Obviously, Frederick and Priscilla were acquainted.

"Really? Let me see the picture again," Roland said, squinting his eyes and bringing the picture close to his face before passing it along to Harold.

"Huh. Well, look at that. Harold, you do look like your father, don't you? How does he look now?"

"Let me see," Harold said. "That is him, alright. Time has not been kind to my father. Or, better said, the amount of drugs and duration of isolation forced upon Frederick have not been kind to him," Harold admitted as he pulled his phone out of his pocket.

"I've been doing my best to restore his dignity. If I can find him at all, he likes sitting at the kitchen table or in the library to work on math problems. Sometimes, he disappears, and the security cameras are useless as there is no record of his activity. Odd, indeed. Nonetheless, I took a picture of some of his work. See? Doesn't it look like a legitimate engineering plan? Plus, he said the name Priscilla just the other day."

"Indeed it does," Astrid agreed, approaching the protrusion in the wall to show Harold. "This drawing here looks to be the same square shape as this perfectly geometrical imperfection in the wall. When I glide my hand back and forth as if checking for imperfections in a yard of expensive fabric, I can tell that the bump does not align with any part of the frame. Can we remove the drywall? Did your dad say anything else when he said Priscilla?"

"Astrid, I already told you. Dad and I worked on that wall and found no way to correct the imperfection. Let us leave the remodeling alone and stick with maintenance," Roland interrupted.

"He also said, 'Hidden. Stolen. Lost,'" Harold answered.

Astrid nodded, "For now, I will agree that maintenance is the priority and an endeavor all in itself. Unfortunately, maintenance can appear as if there is no forward progress, but should you stop, everything backslides, weeds pop up, and the soil has no nutrient replenishment. You know the adage, 'Prevention is better than correction?' Well, it seems that we find correction more exciting as human beings and thus have an entire world history repeating the same story with different characters, locations, and customs."

"Astrid, you just gave me an idea!" Harold exclaimed.

"What would you think about reserving time for Frederick to come in and see your shop? I'll pay you whatever you request to close down The Bee's Knees for two hours so he can have privacy. Maybe if you show him that picture, he will say a helpful word or two."

"I would be honored to do that for your dad. Shall we plan on tomorrow at 2:00 PM?" Astrid offered.

"We shall," answered Harold.

A few seconds later, Lottie came flying with shopping bags, fizzy drinks, and cookies in hand.

Truth Spectacles

Astrid, who had reserved The Bee's Knees as planned, opened her door and waited for the Braggarts with a smile and a wave, "Good morning, Mr. Braggart and Mr. Braggart."

"Hello, Miss Beeswax. Your dress reminds me of my old skateboard and the first time I tried your biscotti," Harold said, referring to their maiden encounter.

"Does it?" Astrid asked as she closed and locked the door and hung the 'Closed' sign. The day's outfit was a 1950s green and white gingham shirtdress: a fitted bodice closed with three evenly spaced button bows, a full A-line skirt, and a slim belt. A sunny yellow bowler hat sat joyfully tilted atop her ebony hair, the back curled under and the front coiffed in two large victory curls. Sunny yellow wedges adorned her feet, and bubblegum pink rosebud earrings added a cheerful accent.

"Please, come in and look around, Frederick. I am

honored to have you here."

Frederick kept looking down at the tattered, flat gray cap in his hands as he hovered near the casement window. Then, he glanced up and saw the black and white vinyl floor, the mint green walls, the orbs of light in their crocheted nets, the antique radio, rotary phone, and cash register, and his eyes changed from distant and hazy to intelligent, observant, and curious. He straightened his shoulders and held his head high, and his expressionless facial features became animated. Within moments, the Frederick of long ago returned and thought The Bee's Kees was The Stealthy Picaroon, and Astrid her Aunt Priscilla.

"Priscilla!" While taking Astrid by the hand, he said,

"How I have missed you! Did your mother make you a new dress? I haven't seen this one before, and I admire all your dresses and categorize them by your mood. I know how bizarre that sounds, and I risk sounding like I left my senses at home, but facts are facts that can only be categorized to be understood. Green means you are hopeful, red equates emotionally conflicted or Christmas, pink means flirtatious and open to advances from male admirers, of which I am first in line, and so the list goes on. The only color you don't wear is brown. Now, Charles, Aloysius, and Oswald promised to meet me here in the next half an hour. Have you retrieved the blueprints and spectacles from the safe? The competition is less than forty-eight hours away. If we want to win, we must successfully add the capstone feature that updates the spectacles with new developments and scientific discoveries so everyone can have the Truth."

Surprised, Astrid stalled with a smile, looked at the protrusion in the wall, remembered the picture of Frederick's drawing on Harold's phone, and answered, "Not yet, I'm afraid."

Frederick shook his head, exhaling exasperatedly, "Priscilla, my beautifully brilliant Priscilla. I gave you instructions, and I expect my instructions to be followed. We don't have time to waste."

"You are right. We do not have time to waste, nor do I want to leave our project out for any passerby to see. I have been alone with customers all day, so I must beg your forgiveness, though please know that my decision was not an oversight but an intentional protective measure," Astrid explained.

Frederick nodded, "Very well, all is forgiven. What cannot be forgiven is the utter disregard for another's time manifested by Oswald every day of his life. Oswald must be reminded that the universe does not orbit around his timetable or distinct lack thereof.

Can you imagine functioning in such a haphazard way? Never mind the last question. May I have the use of your phone? I better call to see if he has left his house. Aloysius and Charles too, for that matter.

If they were as eager as I to become world-renowned inventors, one would think they would not need a swift kick in the rear to be where they say they will be."

"Of course, you may. Let me write down their phone numbers for you," Astrid said, grabbing a light blue notepad and writing them down in reverse alphabetical order.

"I have their phone numbers memorized," Frederick growled as he marched to the telephone and grabbed the receiver like it had offended his ancestors back one thousand generations.

"Very well. I was not calling your intelligence into question, so you have no reason to point your angry arrows in my direction," Astrid retorted, slapping the notepad before him. "Aloysius changed his number recently, so I advise you to use the one I wrote down rather than the one in your memory."

"Hey, Dad," Harold said before clapping his hand over his mouth and widening his eyes in helpless anxiety over his immediate slip of the tongue. Thankfully, Frederick was much too involved in rehearsing the finer points of time management while dialing the rotary phone to notice.

Harold's clap caught Astrid's attention, and she watched his expressions vacillate between a flicker of hope and consuming fear.

She imagined what might be going through his

mind as the scene unfolded. What would his dad think when, or if, he ever realized that he was talking to his son? Would he revert to his previous state or stay where he was, in his twenties, and set on becoming a world-renowned inventor? Would he come into the present and understand the years and events that had passed? Had Frederick any lucid moments at home?

Aiming to snap Harold back into the moment, Astrid whispered, "Go outside and call Roland to inform him that Frederick will be calling under the assumption that Roland is Aloysius."

Harold nodded but could not tear his eyes away from his father. Astrid leaned against his arm, giving him a playful shove with her hip.

"Yep. I mean, yes. I will call him right now."

When Roland answered the phone, his native melancholy tendencies sounded louder than they had the previous day, "Hey, Harold. Did you and your dad already visit The Bee's Knees?"

"Yes, we are visiting right now, in fact. Listen, we have a critical situation. A few moments after we got here, Frederick came back from wherever he has been and thinks that he is inside the Stealthy Picaroon, that Astrid is your Aunt Priscilla, and Aloysius, Mr. Pip, and Oswald are part of his invention team.

From what he has said so far, the drawings and math problems he did the other day are part of

something that really did exist. Astrid gave him your phone number, so make up a good story for Aloysius's absence."

Roland paused briefly to digest the information.

"Did you hear me? I'm looking through the window, and he looks like he's about to end his current conversation. I would not want to be on the receiving end of that jaw," Harold said.

"I heard you, yes, and was pondering my options, the best of which seems to be acquiring my father's name and persona," Roland said.

"How are you going to pull that off?" Harold asked.

"Easier than you might think. I'm at my mother's, helping her through her second round of old boxes. A few of Dad's old sweaters have survived and are of a reasonably acceptable appearance to be worn in public. I'll put one on and be on my way," Roland said.

"Thank you. Is Lottie with you? I would love to have her look at Frederick's drawings and give us her professional opinion," Harold said.

"She is at a work conference, but if you text her the picture, she can analyze it," Roland offered.

"Great idea. Thanks again, and see you soon," Harold said, ending the call, sending a text, and taking a few minutes to check Moose University track and field stats to calm his frayed nerves while

Frederick finished his phone calls.

When he walked back inside, Frederick was showering Astrid with condescending compliments, "Your eyes remind me of a seductive feline who waits and lets their victims put themselves in hazardous situations before attacking. And, as I said before, you are brilliant, though one could easily overlook your brilliance if enchanted by your lips and the way you move your hands when you talk, like an ethereal and intoxicating dream weaver."

"Oh, Frederick, as smitten as I may or may not be with your unique flatteries, we have more important matters at hand. Are the Three Musketeers on their way?" Astrid asked, careful to avoid recent cultural references.

He rolled his eyes, "The Three Musketeers, indeed—'all for one and one for all. United, we stand. Divided we fall,' as Alexander Dumas penned."

"I suppose Three Musketeers doesn't quite work, seeing as there are four of you," Astrid said, correcting herself.

Thankfully, before she offended Frederick further, Roland walked in wearing an old argyle sweater, his unruly hair coiffed into one large curl, straight jeans, and black and white Converse high-top sneakers.

"Hello, my wonderful sister. Hello Freddy. Am I

late?" Roland said with a smile and a wink.

"You are right on time. Oswald and Charles both sounded surprised when I called like we hadn't held this weekly meeting since we were freshmen in college," Frederick said through clenched teeth. "I reminded them that we have less than forty-eight hours to work out our glitch and to get their hind parts down here. Charles apologized profusely, and Oswald was confused, which tells you how little this means to him. He then proceeded to give me a detailed accounting of a new bolt he found and other irrelevant anecdotes. We might as well forfeit the winnings right now for how dependable Oswald is."

"They'll be here soon," Roland said, directing Frederick's attention to the tulips and roses.

"Astrid," Harold whispered as he touched her elbow and nodded toward the table in the back corner. "Can we talk for a moment?"

"Yes, I have a back room that will afford us privacy. However, before I let you enter my sanctuary, I must swear you to secrecy regarding its contents, and under no conditions are you to comment on what you do or do not see," Astrid instructed.

"You have my word," Harold said, touching his heart.

***

While Astrid enjoyed the privilege of her own room

and held sway over decorating decisions in the Beeswax home, she couldn't shake the feeling that it was still primarily her mother's domain. Though The Bee's Knees belonged to her as a flower shop, its focus remained on serving its clientele. Consequently, the shop's backroom became a space she could genuinely claim as her own. Surprisingly spacious, it rivaled the main floral shop in size and served as her haven.

One wall boasted a vintage cherry wood bookcase, its glass doors and brass handles showcasing Astrid's beloved classics, each lovingly rebound in hardcovers of her design. Despite her modesty in displaying only her handmade cards at her store, Astrid's artistic prowess, honed through numerous art lessons from Beatrice, was evident in her intricate work. Her preference for swirly metallic lettering, vibrant hues, and whimsical designs imbued her creations with her unique charm.

Adjacent to the bookcase, a drawing desk stood proudly, adorned with an array of art supplies meticulously organized in boxes and jars. Colored pencils, fine-tipped markers, watercolors, and everything needed to facilitate Astrid's creative endeavors stood at the ready. Unknown to anyone but Astrid and Lottie, this facade of artistic expression hid the clandestine workshop of the bumblebee listening devices. Her favorite amenities included a cozy brown chair nestled by a gas fireplace and a small but fully functioning kitchen.

"Welcome," Astrid said as she observed her room from an outsider's perspective, noticing the imperfections anew: a crack along one floorboard, an old nail hole, and four days' worth of dust on a reading lamp.

"I'm sorry that my father is expressing romantic interest in you and making uncomfortable comments," Harold began.

"Don't worry about me. How are you doing?" Astrid asked.

"Truthfully, I have a lot of thoughts. My father appears lucid, but who knows if his words have any foundation. Maybe what he is talking about never happened, and this is an alternate reality he has imagined for decades. Roland entering the building as Aloysius might be helpful or prove disastrous. Mr. Pip's and Oswald's decisions will elicit the same. What will he do when he looks in the mirror and sees he is old? Or steps outside into a world full of technology and information all of which he has never seen or heard of before? Does he remember anything that has happened throughout the years? How strong do you think he is? And how fragile?" Harold said, rubbing his temples with his fingers.

"Mentally or physically?" Astrid asked.

"Both," Harold replied.

"Which one is first on your mind?"

"In this case, the two cannot be separated," Harold said.

Astrid studied Harold briefly before gently touching his arm, "You are right on that point. Why don't we see what Mr. Pip and Oswald know and go from there? The future requires what we are learning in the present."

"Why does that suggestion seem so unhelpful? I know you are right; I was hoping for instant desired results and a fortune teller's crystal ball," Harold sighed, leaning against the bookcase and accidentally knocking down a few books.

"Let me pick those up," Astrid said, gracefully kneeling and quickly collecting the books in her arms.

"I am so sorry. Can I help put them back?" Harold asked, kneeling next to Astrid and noticing that the perfectly straight corners of one of the books were newly bent by the fall. "The book you are holding in your left hand is damaged, so I will order a new one right now. What is the title?"

"*A Framework for Understanding Poverty* by Ruby K. Payne. Please do not buy another one as I have already highlighted and written in this copy and hardly have the time to transfer my thoughts to a new one. Bent corners hardly change the value of a book anyway, and I must request that you do not have one shipped anonymously as if I will not know who sent it," Astrid said, blushing.

"Very well, I will respect your wishes and avoid purchasing that particular book," Harold said, smiling and mentally noting ideas for the future.

***

As Mr. Pip pulled his old blue Chevy truck into a parking spot in front of The Bee's Knees, Oswald came down the sidewalk, blinking rapidly as if trying to dislodge an eyelash from his eye.

"Oswald," said Mr. Pip, stepping out of his truck and combing his bushy white mustache with a tiny blue comb.

"Mr. Pippy Pants," said Oswald with a snide grin. "I see you are using a toy comb intended for toy ponies to comb your obnoxious mustache."

"I'm glad to hear that your glasses are working well," Mr. Pip said as he finished his combing ritual. "I never thought we would enter this building together again, but here we are."

"Here we are, indeed. Shall I enter first, or shall you?" Oswald asked.

"Genius first," Mr. Pip said, opening the door and waiting for Oswald to pass.

"Freddy! We apologize for our delay, for we know the matter at hand is an urgent one," Mr. Pip said, entering behind Oswald.

"Where is Priscilla? Priscilla! Priscilla!" Frederick

roared, ignoring his friends.

Astrid came running around the corner, "Yes, Frederick?"

"Now that we're all assembled, and I trust this serves as the final reminder regarding the importance of punctuality, let's proceed with our tasks," Frederick declared, gesturing toward the entrance of Astrid's sanctuary and marching in without permission.

With a few determined pushes, he nudged the vintage bookcase, revealing a concealed compartment tall enough to accommodate a person if they were kneeling. A metal safe, firmly anchored to the floor, occupied the recess beyond the opening, explaining why the opposite wall could never achieve a flush appearance. Undeterred, Frederick advanced, deftly unlocking the safe with a combination etched indelibly into his memory despite the passage of time and the influence of countless medications. From within, he extracted a bundle of blueprints and a meticulously crafted jewelry box, fashioned from rich mahogany and adorned with an intricate, hand-painted bumblebee motif, its surface gleaming with a polished lacquer finish.

When he carried them to the table in the main lobby, Mr. Pip and Oswald's eyes widened, and their mouths hung partially open. Only then did they officially acknowledge the other as anything more than an irritant. Roland was unaffected and

pretended that a hidden safe was no more intriguing than a drop of rain.

"As you all know, we are about to change the world for everyone, especially for those who suffer from sicknesses of the mind," Frederick said, unable to successfully open the jewelry box.

"Shall we stop whatever is about to unfold?" Astrid asked Harold. "I can feign hysteria or go fetch Nova from school. She'll put an end to all privacy and contemplative quietness in under three seconds."

"No, no," Harold said as a distracted afterthought while his attention was riveted by the goings on before him.

"If we don't stop this, circumstances may become bigger than we are prepared for. I'm serious about feigning hysteria for your benefit. I have a scream that can make others scream; it sounds that harrowing," Astrid said.

Harold smiled weakly, "I appreciate your generosity. But he has his senses right now. Who knows, maybe this is the beginning of his permanent return. He might remember Adelaide, me, Ingrid, what happened to him over the years that cannot be accounted for. I know that you are trying to protect me, but my family has been undone for a long time. There is no new revelation that could make things worse."

"He doesn't have his senses, Harold. He has

memories," Astrid replied with a sad smile of her own.

"Priscilla!" Frederick said, demanding her attention and pointing toward her sanctuary. "The jewelry box is locked, and you are the only one with the key. I saw it hanging on your wall. Go get it, and next time, you should not be so conspicuous."

"See here, I am not your maid nor butler. Your legs and feet work as well as mine, so why don't you solve your own problem and retrieve it yourself?" Astrid snapped.

"Priscilla used to do everything he said," Mr. Pip whispered as he picked up his tiny comb that he purposefully dropped on the ground. "I know you are not Priscilla, but you might play the part until we see where this is going. If he loses his temper, whatever this is, is over."

"Since you are clearly on the rag, I shall forgive your obstinacy," Frederick said.

"Whatever would I do without your unrivaled benevolence? Forgive me, for you are once again correct. The plight of all women has come upon me and severed my reasoning skills. I forgot I am subservient, docile, without logic or half of my brain. Or is it my liver? What organ resides in my skull? Please accept my humble and unquestioning obedience as penance for my sins," Astrid said, bowing slightly forward.

Harold pretended his laugh was a cough and turned around to get a drink of water.

"I was only asking you to get the keys," Frederick said, perplexed and still pointing.

Astrid refrained from pointing out that he had commanded, not requested, her assistance. Instead, she followed the direction of his finger to a collection of knickknacks and trinkets once cherished by her grandma. Among them was a delicate white wicker birdcage adorned with silk flowers suspended from an elegant white stand. A vintage door knocker, intricately engraved with roses, was mounted on the wall, accompanied by four slender steel keys dangling from a steel ring. It was only upon closer inspection that Astrid noticed the ornate initials gracing the end of each key: A.B., P.B., J.I., and F.B.

Despite the temptation to seize the keys and flee to prevent the disaster that was surely on its way, Astrid maintained her composure. Frederick's demeanor offered no assurance of trustworthiness as his restless gaze and frenetic thoughts betrayed him.

"Do you think anyone is watching us?" Frederick asked the group of men as he began looking in every corner and lifting every vase. "Priscilla, do hurry over here with the keys!"

Astrid handed the key ring to Frederick's trembling-with-excitement hands as everyone in

the room waited to see what was in store. With a gentle click, the jewelry box opened. Lined with mint green velvet and a faux pearl strand along the bottom edges, the gem repository was entirely empty.

"Where are the spectacles?" Frederick's voice sliced through the air as it crackled with tension. His accusatory tone pierced the room like a sharp blade.

"Priscilla, where are the spectacles? You assured me they were secured. Have you dared to breach the sanctity of our trust? Are you conspiring with the enemy and divulging our secrets? You've betrayed us. I knew you couldn't be trusted. Pip, Oswald, Aloysius! We have a traitor in our midst." As his glare intensified, his face contorted into a visage of scathing rage and wounded pride.

"Excuse me, sir, but I am not in the habit of being spoken to like an insubordinate worker bee. I know no more about the whereabouts of the spectacles than you, and if you ever accuse me of treachery again, I shall refuse to let you set foot in my establishment. Do I make myself clear?" Astrid said as she gripped the table's edge and leaned slightly forward, glaring.

Frederick glared right back, undeterred and increasingly losing control, "Treachery? Who are you to speak of treachery? You smile prettily and blink your emerald eyes whenever you want anything from anyone. You do it to me, Oswald,

Charles, and you would do the same to Aloysius if he weren't your brother. You know I love you, yet you stand before me beside this man I have never seen. Is his name Square John Dullsville? What secrets did you promise him? Clearly, from the look in his eyes, he is smitten with you.

You gave him our spectacles, didn't you? And now, you bring him before me to mock me!" Frederick screamed louder as spittle flew from his mouth. He flung the table on its side, grabbed a nearby vase, raised it above his head, and hurled it with all his might in Astrid's direction.

Astrid screamed. Harold grabbed her around the waist and turned just in time for the vase to hit his shoulder, breaking into pieces. One shard flew over Harold and slashed down Astrid's cheek like shrapnel in a war zone.

Blood began to flow. Frederick froze.

Roland was quickly beside Frederick, talking calmly, "Hey, Freddy. We'll find the spectacles. Priscilla has never given any inclination of betrayal. Square John Dullsville, as you so affectionately called him, is our childhood friend here for a visit. That's it. I've never seen him try to invent anything in my life, and as far as I know, his strengths lie in delegation and persuasion."

Oswald and Mr. Pip picked up the table, nodded, and each brought out a case of Asteroid Mints and offered one to Frederick. He took one from each, slowly settled himself into a chair, and put his head in his hands. "Not again," he whispered as he began to cry. "How could I lose control like that again? Priscilla, I am so sorry. Forgive me."

Facial wounds and head wounds always produce copious amounts of blood, which is precisely what the laceration on Astrid's face did. Blood ran down her neck, staining her green gingham dress. Tears threatened to flow, but she held them back as she pressed her palm to her cheek and searched for her first aid kit.

"Let me see it?" Harold asked.

"No, I'm sure it's fine. I'll step into the bathroom and clean it up. After I apply a couple of butterfly band-aids, I'll be as good as new," Astrid said with a half-smile.

"'Tis only a scrape."

"Please, let me see your face, Astrid. There is blood running between your fingers," Harold said as he reached up to move her hand.

Astrid didn't resist, and Harold soon saw the long laceration on her high, porcelain cheekbone, "A first aid kit is not going to be sufficient. You need stitches. Keep putting pressure on it until we get you to the hospital."

"My first aid kit might not be sufficient, but Mr. Pip's is. Right, Charles?" Astrid asked as she grabbed a cloth and pressed it to her cheek.

"Yes, as a dentist, ahem, as someone who will soon be a dentist, I am prepared," Mr. Pip said. "I'll just go out to my car and grab my bag."

Frederick's eyes darted around the room, landing his accusatory gaze on Harold, "Why are you calling Priscilla, Astrid? And why is Priscilla addressing Charles as 'Mr. Pip' as if he were several decades her elder? And why does Oswald look like he has aged a century overnight while still sporting that absurd haircut? You're the one responsible for all this, aren't you? If you weren't here, I would not be losing my mind. If I had my spectacles, I could put them on and see the Truth! All I want is the Truth!" Frederick leaned down, picked up a piece of the broken vase, squeezed it in his hand, stood, and lunged at Harold.

Harold reacted instinctively, shielding Astrid behind him as he raised his arm to block Frederick's attack. Roland caught Frederick by the back of his shirt and pulled him back toward the chair, restraining him as he kicked and bit. "Get Astrid out of here!" he yelled.

Witnessing anyone, especially a loved one, enter the beginning stages of psychosis is frightening. What can be said? What can be done? Once a course of action is decided, each person must make the secondary decision of being at peace with unintended consequences, comforting themselves with knowing that they did the best with what they had at the time. Now, imagine the exponential agony of a child watching their parent who has been intellectually absent for decades coming around to what appears to be complete clarity. Harold's moment of hope for the future was followed by the sickening realization that his hopes were false, foolish, and devastatingly foiled.

His heart felt as if it had been strapped forcefully onto a roller coaster that went as high as the rising sun only to plummet back to the ground at breakneck speed. The ground, with its dirt and pollution, and the claustrophobic sensation of knowing that the next step will follow the predictable, unchangeable drudgery.

"I never should have brought him here. I am so sorry," Harold said to Astrid as he kept a protective arm around her and guided her to the back room. "Go inside your sanctuary, lock the door, and wait for one of us to call you. Do you have your phone?"

"Yes, I have my phone, and I do not need you to worry about me. I can handle myself," Astrid protested.

"I am not calling your resilience and tenacity into question. I am asking you to remember that Frederick thinks you're Priscilla. Right now, he is a danger to himself and others. You need immediate medical attention, and Roland won't last much longer," Harold said as he saw his heartbreak mirrored in the eyes of his friend.

"Alright, I'll sequester myself in my sanctuary, though if I must sequester by myself by demand,

then the sanctuary title no longer fits. Furthermore . . ." Astrid began.

"Thank you," Harold said before turning around to do what needed to be done.

Oswald, Mr. Pip, and Old Grievances

The removal of Frederick from The Bee's Knees was heartbreaking. The minute Astrid disappeared from Frederick's view, his dynamic brown eyes lost their dimension of intelligence and curiosity. They became flat, black saucers— eyes that could look but couldn't see. Harold pulled up a chair beside him and asked Frederick if he could help him to the truck.

"What do you think? Should we get back to the plants?" Harold asked one more time in a steady voice, holding out his open hand, palm up, while trying to ignore the uncontrollable tears flowing down his face. "Back to the plants. Things that start with the letter *p* get lost in dirt," Frederick whispered, his head slightly forward. He stood, staring once again at the flat gray cap in his hand, and refused to take another step despite encouragement and pleadings from Mr. Pip,

Oswald, and Harold. Roland remained silent.

The more emotion crept into their voices, the more rigid Frederick became until he quite took on the appearance of a statue.

"What do you want to do, Harold?" Roland asked.

"I don't know. This cannot be happening, and for the record, I no longer believe in rock bottom," Harold replied, exhausted. "We could pick him up, I guess."

"We could. Or, we could call 911," Roland said.

"No, I do not want to take him to the hospital where the noises, smells, and apathetic staff will worsen his condition. He needs his familiar surroundings, and he will be back to normal—well, his normal," Harold explained.

"He might get a caring and compassionate doctor and nurse," Roland suggested.

"Unlikely," Mr. Pip uttered softly. "Last week, when I went to the hospital to pick up a friend, they referred to her by a number, not by her name. When people lose their humanity in the eyes of the very institution trying to help them, they feel it in their soul, even if they cannot speak."

"Let's help him to the truck. He has a caring and compassionate doctor who will meet me at the house," Harold explained.

So, they put their arms around Frederick, and Harold drove him. By the time they arrived, Harold had no tears left to cry.

***

While The Bee's Knees occupants waited for Harold to return, Mr. Pip cleansed and stitched up Astrid's wound. "I suspect you will have an impressive scar for a bit. What will you tell people when they ask what happened?" he asked.

"I shall tell them that I fell upon an ice skate while in pursuit of a fox who stole a pie from my window," Astrid said with a smirk.

"What if they ask follow-up questions?" Harold asked as he re-entered the floral shop.

"I'll list the ingredients for berry pie and describe each item in such detail that the inquiring party will regret asking their question," she said with a shrug. "How is your father?"

"Thankfully, he is with Dr. Sereneheart. Beyond that, I have no idea. What does 'fine' even measure in these situations? Don't answer that. How are you? At least you have stopped bleeding," Harold observed.

"My wound will heal in no time. As for what we all witnessed this afternoon, Oswald and Mr. Pip, you two are the only ones who know the details and history of the spectacles and Priscilla's involvement. Please, I implore you to disclose all

you know right now, even if it puts someone in an unfavorable light. Does our mother know anything about this? If she does, she might as well be here, too," Astrid said.

"Your mother was not around during the inauguration of this failed experiment. Whether Aloysius told her after they met, we have no way of knowing. What we can tell you is these blueprints are clever forgeries. See, Charles? If you paid as much attention to detail as you claim to do, you would have noticed when we put them in the safe," Oswald said as he pointed to the flattened blueprints on the table.

"My work? Attention to detail? I examined every inch of those documents for hints of forgery in accordance with our group agreement that all involved would leave the authentic blueprints at The Stealthy Picaroon to prevent theft. You would have been just as fruitless, and you know it," Mr. Pip retorted.

"History proves that the weak link in all this was you, always worrying about feelings and hidden meanings. I said deal with the facts; the facts never lie," Oswald affirmed with a haughty tone.

"And your opinion was the problem, was it not? Facts can be misunderstood and misrepresented, which opens the door for deception and distraction, the very pitfalls we were trying to prevent by creating the spectacles in the first place. Then, you had to pretend that logic was the gold standard, as if humankind fought wars, loved, grieved, and pursued the seemingly impossible because it was logical to do so. Your complete disregard for human emotion essentially opened the door to failure," Mr. Pip said, digging in his pocket for his tiny mustache comb.

"Still using your pacifier, are you?" Oswald taunted.

"Okay, you two. The bickering can end," Roland interrupted before Mr. Pip's red face led to his internal combustion. "Please, tell us about the reality-check spectacles from the beginning."

"How is your arm?" Oswald asked.

"Well, I have been using my left arm, but I will likely need an ice pack and pain medication when I get home. Now, please, tell us the story," Roland pressed.

After a few deep breaths, the two men nodded in agreement and told their origin story.

***

Aloysius, Charles, Frederick, and Oswald met during their freshman year at Moose University. During the first fall semester, there was a fire in the dorms. Some imbeciles put a lighted candle on the windowsill next to the curtains. The curtains went up in flames, setting off the alarm. They didn't share rooms or even know each other before that, but being out in the freezing cold rain in the middle of a November night trying to save lives, property, and sanity accelerates the get-to-know-your-community process.

Thankfully, no one died, but the building needed extensive repairs before being deemed habitable again. Moose University rented nearby homes to house students while they waited, and the four men were assigned to the same large room with a set of bunk beds on either side.

They quickly discovered that they all shared one personality quirk: an unrelenting concern and ability to identify problems and offer solutions. Innovation and invention, if you will. Given their age and ignorance of the language of passive academia, the only people who took them seriously were themselves. The other men quickly understood that Frederick was a luminary mathematician ensnared within the relentless grip of mental afflictions. His journey was tumultuous, where the battle to retain his cognitive faculties transcended the ordinary bounds of perseverance.

In moments of frenzied vigor, he wielded his intellect like a blazing comet, achieving feats that ordinarily demanded weeks or months in a mere flicker of time. Yet, this brilliance was a double-edged sword, for lurking in the shadows were unseen phantoms, malicious spirits that tormented him relentlessly.

Despite their spectral nature, their toll upon his being was palpable, etched into his handsome face.

In his relentless pursuit for respite, Frederick conceived of a visionary solution— a pair of spectacles imbued with the power of reality based on complex algorithms. He called them Truth Spectacles.

Through these lenses, he hoped to placate the demons that besieged his troubled mind and to filter what was reality and what was not. His ambitions knew no bounds, envisioning lenses that would bestow upon him the wisdom of the ages: the Latin appellations of flora and fauna, the arcane mysteries of weather patterns, the flux of housing markets, the pulse of athletic realms, the intricacies of anatomy and physiology.

While Frederick worked on algorithms, Oswald lent his penchant for noticing patterns and details, retaining facts as if he were Encyclopedia Britannica, contributing an endless stream of information. Mr. Pip worked on the functionality and comfort of the frames, and Aloysius researched various mental health conditions to streamline the purpose of the information.

All the men needed was a private and secure workplace, which Priscilla provided inside the walls of The Stealthy Picaroon, always serving refreshments and encouragement.

Priscilla's world was small by design, as she was neither adventurous nor inclined to go to public places. She often said, "Some people have a peg leg. I have a peg brain. Would you insist that someone with an amputated arm attempt to hold water in two hands? Then, why must you insist I do what I cannot do?"

The men were racing to finish their Truth Spectacles for the Inventive Assemblage, a competitive and prestigious competition for hopeful innovators. That year, there would be a substantial cash prize, sponsorship opportunities, and the potential for cross-continental travel. Frederick wasn't interested in the money since he had enough to fund whatever project he wanted, but the others were in want of money to pay for otherwise impossible opportunities. Yet, Frederick was a Braggart in more than name regarding his intellectual acuity. He saw his mission as ethically superior, convincing himself that he could disregard everyone else whenever he wanted.

***

"If our prototype had been successfully fitted with the upgrade feature we designed, our invention truly would have been the bee's knees," Oswald explained.

"You cannot help yourself, can you?" Mr. Pip asked with an eye roll before returning his attention to Astrid.

"On the day we tested the upgrade feature, Frederick had one of his rage attacks. Each successive test was a failure, and we were all stressed out, bickering, and fatigued from too many late nights. Usually, if we ignored Frederick, he would yell a few offensive words, storm off, and come back several hours later, apologizing for his behavior. But that night he started throwing our paperwork around, speaking English but not making sense."

"He grabbed his car keys, slammed the door, and peeled out of his parking spot like a maniac. Pippy Pants over here asked Priscilla to go to his estate to talk some sense into him as he was the crowning piece of our invention. I advised against it since Priscilla was known to panic when outside her well-constructed universe. The dark frightened her, Frederick frightened her, and driving frightened her. She was no match for Frederick in his agitated state because she always and forevermore considered the feelings of others before her safety, and he would rail against her worse than anyone else, as we witnessed today. We could, and did, take his verbal assaults and give them no more heed. But, Priscilla? Her tender heart was wounded repeatedly. It's a fact that Frederick often would return to himself quicker with her than with anyone else. So, she sacrificed the very part of herself that made her Priscilla to keep everyone happy because that is the kind of person she was. That was the last night we saw her, alive or dead. We can thank Mr. Pip for that."

Mr. Pip looked down and hung his head. "To my everlasting shame, what Oswald says is true. I asked her to go. I wanted Frederick to return so we could finish our project, and I was too impatient to wait out his predictable course of action. I would never have asked if I had known that she would disappear."

"But you knew that you were asking her to do things that caused her great anxiety," Oswald protested. "The last time she drove in a car by herself at night, she wound up bedridden for three days, refusing to eat. What did you expect?"

"Gentleman, please, you are casting aspersions in the wrong direction, and none of us are the better for it. What did our dad think of his sister running such an errand?" Roland inquired, voicing Astrid's question as well as his own.

"Aloysius was never one to tell anyone what to do. Priscilla eagerly agreed to go as she, too, believed that her intervention was the most helpful course of action. He asked her if she thought it was in her best interest to go three or four times with as much variation. When she walked out the door, his eyes were full of worry, but he did not try to stop her," Oswald said, the venom slowly leaving his voice.

"What was my dad's response to learning of Priscilla's disappearance?" Harold asked.

"He returned the next day, completely calm and distantly apologetic. He denied ever seeing Priscilla when we asked how their visit went. We assumed a visit had occurred since he had returned to the polite and reasonable version of himself. Frederick's demeanor was so apathetic it was both out of character and disturbing. For a man full of turbulent passion in general and romantic feelings for Priscilla, he was numb," Mr. Pip explained.

"Or, he appeared numb to feeling," Astrid noted. "Reactions to loss can be unpredictable. In my view, if he appeared numb at the outset, he probably knew before any of you came undone and managed his grief, or guilt, by pretending he was unaffected."

"I'm sorry, Astrid, but did you just say guilt?" Harold said as anger and sadness danced across his features in equal measure. "That came out more accusatory than intended; I apologize."

Astrid stepped closer to Harold, touched his arm with both hands, and spoke gently, "I am not suggesting guilt to wound you or your dad. However, if his moods and perceptions swung as wide as is being described, and as we saw today, he could have said or done something while out of control."

Harold fought the temptation to rip his arm away from Astrid, yell hurtful words he couldn't take back, speed home, and demand answers from a man who didn't know who he was. Instead, he asked, "What did Aloysius do when he realized his sister would never be found?'

Mr. Pip explained, "The presumption of death certificate was slow in coming, yet Aloysius maintained his native cheery temperament, hoping that each subsequent hour would be the hour Priscilla returned to The Stealthy Picaroon. Once the facts demanded acknowledgment, he was heartbroken, though never accusatory. He and his parents closed the candy shop, boarded the windows, and locked the doors. Frederick married Adelaide within months without explanation; we didn't even know who she was. Aloysius married Beatrice, Oswald opened his toy shop, and I went to dental school."

"None of us had a coherent conversation with Frederick ever again. We had nothing left to talk about," Oswald added. "Pippy Pants sent the only woman I have ever loved to her death, and that sin is unforgivable. If he had been patient and waited twelve hours or three days, or however long it would have taken Frederick to come to his senses, we might have had the spectacles and Priscilla. Or, we may never have had the spectacles, but we would have Priscilla. Now we have neither."

"I am too old and too tired to argue. Condemn me if you must, Oswald, but know that I have held myself in contempt these many years, and not even you can serve as a harsher judge," Mr. Pip said as he lowered himself slowly into a white wicker chair with a pink covered cushion. "My only condolence in life is the little girl I now raise as my own. I pray to God that I do not fail her, too."

Oswald teared up and swallowed the harsh words that sprang into his mouth as his chest deflated, "Truth be told, Charles, I hold myself responsible, too. I didn't try to stop her and couldn't have if I had tried. I am sorry for the decades of silence between us, the lost friendship, and the harm I have caused you. If you can find it in your heart to forgive me, perhaps I can forgive you, too. Then, perhaps we can forgive ourselves."

Mr. Pip stood once more, wiped his eyes, and looked at his old friend, remembering him for everything he was rather than what he wasn't. "Very well, may forgiveness abound, though I must point out that forgiveness is a gift given rather than a trade made. Now that we have freed up the energy required to hold grudges, let us solve the case of Priscilla Beeswax if we are to be of any help to Harold in his time of need. Did you see his eyes at the end?"

"I saw them the entire time. Well, almost the entire time. I imagine the last scene was devastating," Astrid said, shaking the image out of her head. "Here is a picture Roland found in one of Mama's old boxes."

She became so enraptured by the sight of old grievances and assumptions being laid to rest that she twirled on her heel three times, hugged both men, and handed them the photo of Priscilla, "We can all find her together! None of us can do what lies ahead alone."

"Millie is holding her Easter brunch soon, which will be an excellent place to gather information. She knew Priscilla, as did many of her guests,"

Oswald suggested.

"Excellent idea! You two must pretend as if you still hate each other. Experience has taught me nothing excites conversation like assumptions void of objective or subjective evidence," Astrid said.

"Millie's current hot topic is arguing about increased funding for the Board of Education. Note that she does not argue for increased funding, only about it. If we stir the pot on the issue, one of us can bring up Priscilla's great crusade for equal opportunity library privileges from our college days, to which Mrs. Duncecap was opposed. If her feathers get ruffled, she'll tell you everything she knows," Mr. Pip said.

"And then I can ask her all sorts of questions," Astrid replied. "You are correct. The offended tend to cultivate a list of their offender's weaknesses, quirks, and mistakes. If Mrs. Duncecap follows her predictable pattern, we will better understand who Priscilla was and who outside the Spectacle Circle may have wanted to harm her. Harold, you must attend as my date."

"Gladly," Harold agreed.

"She didn't have enemies," Oswald pointed out. "She was kind to everyone."

"My working hypothesis is that someone other than the members of the Spectacle Circle knew the details of the project and hovered outside the window, waiting for an opportunity. When

Frederick stormed out, they followed him. Priscilla may have walked in on an argument; she was killed, her body disposed of, and the guilty party walked away, with Frederick unable to do anything for reasons currently unknown. But remember, it's only a hypothesis, and I won't funnel all evidence in that direction if it doesn't fit," Astrid said.

"Harold, did you send the picture of Harold's sketches to Lottie?" Roland asked.

"Yes. I had forgotten about it until now. She says these spectacles have elements of technology that would not have been around all those years ago, like behavioral analysis, voice commands, and Bluetooth connection," Harold reported.

"It seems to me that Frederick never stopped learning. I wonder if Adelaide ever noticed?" Astrid asked.

"She acted as if Frederick was purely an annoyance and a way to keep the family money, but she could easily have had other motives," Harold said.

"I look forward to the day when her name is no longer the center of conversations," Roland said, annoyed.

"Me, too. More importantly, I need to find something to eat," Oswald agreed, opening the door to leave. "Oh! Astrid, Roland, did either of you inherit Aloysius's radio-antenna ears? He could hear a conversation from across the room, other noise and chaos notwithstanding. We had a grand time wreaking havoc on local scuttlebutt with that gift of his."

Harold raised an eyebrow at the question Roland answered without hesitation, "Dad was a one-of-a-kind man, wasn't he?"

"He sure was," Oswald agreed, with a wink.

"Roland, you answered a question with a question," Harold pointed out.

"Did I? Speaking of questions, I have a favor to ask. As you know, I am trying to convince the school to allocate extra funds to make a one-of-a-kind experience for the youth participating in Race Together. Since the idea for the track meet originated with you, and since you are going with Astrid to the Easter brunch, would you mind making one of your convincing speeches if an opportunity presents itself?"

"I'd be happy to, or I can happily pay for whatever you request," Harold offered.

"Thank you, but for various reasons, I think money from alums and donors would make a better impression," Roland said.

"Technically, I am an alum and a donor, but I see your point. Very well, a speech, long-winded comment, or pithy remark shall be made. So, which one of you has this radio-antenna hearing? You might as well tell me."

"Observation is an underappreciated art, I daresay. Recent discoveries are best returned to the safe, wouldn't you agree?" Astrid said as she gathered the materials. "I doubt very much if watching eyes are not still watching."

They all shared one personality quirk: an unrelenting concern and ability to identify problems and offer solutions.

The Easter Brunch

On the day of the brunch, Astrid transformed the local high school gym into a mesmerizing world of spring that smelled as magical as it looked. A magnificent arrangement of roses, peonies, hydrangeas, tulips, and lilies cascaded from a grand crystal vase, creating a lush tapestry of colors and textures. Soft hues of pale pink, lavender, peach, and ivory intermingle harmoniously, evoking a sense of timeless beauty and grace.

Around the table, smaller versions of the centerpiece served as exquisite table accents, bringing bursts of floral splendor to every corner. Miniature roses, delicate peonies, and dainty tulips danced in petite vases, adding a touch of whimsy and charm.

As guests began to take their seats, they were delighted to discover a small posy tied with a powder-blue ribbon resting delicately on each plate. Glittery Easter eggs, artificial soft white bunnies, and fluffy yellow chicks were placed in a classy and conversational way throughout, and to bring a bit of fun to the event, Astrid convinced Millie to set up two porcelain geese dressed in darling green raincoats on either side of her chair. Lottie commented that Millie and the geese were reminiscent of Santa Claus and his elves and wondered if there would be a photographer for anyone wanting to sit on her lap.

"Nearly everyone has a phone with such capabilities. If no one sits on her lap in real-time, they can certainly use artificial intelligence to conjure a rendering," Astrid said, chuckling softly as she affixed bumblebees in and around the geese and flowers.

"I am excited to test out the bumblebee upgrades," Lottie said. "What business are we listening for this time?"

"If you hear the name Priscilla, note anything said before or after. Who knows? Perhaps we shall happen upon a secret alliance."

"How will we know if two people are making a secret alliance?"

"We will know. If it does happen, it will be in a word, a tone, a facial expression, a nod, or, most

tellingly, the immediate pretending of disinterest in each other after the two parties reach an agreement.”

“Huh. I need a nap; all that sounds exhausting.”

“Take a nap if you must, and I will worry about the rest,” Astrid said with a wink.

“You cannot accomplish the mission all by yourself. We are a team, remember? It’s a good thing I wore all white so I could look like a toddler’s napkin by the time I was done eating. Why didn’t you warn me about a chocolate fountain?” Lottie asked.

Her white dress, fated to become stained, had a column silhouette, with buttons down the bodice and eyelet lace around the hem. “I need to run out to the car to grab a couple of things. When is Harold arriving? You are stunning today. Stardust Silhouettes, I assume?” For Astrid and Lottie, compliments were verbal hugs since neither was inclined to unsolicited embraces.

“Yes, soon, and the Spectacle Circle has seven members, so you needn’t worry about me working alone if a nap is in order,” Astrid answered. Her dress was a chiffon A-line made in lavender with hints of pink and white flowers dancing amidst a mock turtleneck, lantern sleeves, and an oversized sash, all trimmed with delicate ivory lace.

Simple pearls adorned her ears, while her hat, tilted jauntily to the side, was of the same lavender with a mint green ribbon tied around the crown accentuated by pearly embellishments and a cluster of fabric flowers in shades of purple, white, and pink reminiscent of a blooming garden. Her mint green pumps were accentuated by three pearls adorning each heel.

Lottie was halfway across the gym floor when she whispered, "Our hostess is coming straight toward you."

Heeding the warning, Astrid stood, spun on her heel, and greeted her client warmly. "Hello, Millie. I do hope I have made your vision a reality."

"I hired you because you are the best; I would not be satisfied if you were not the best. What happened to your face? You look positively terrible," Millie said.

"Why do we say positively terrible rather than negatively terrible if looking terrible is associated with a negative occurrence? If you did not like my work, but other people told you I was the best, would you pretend to like it?" Astrid asked playfully.

"This is no time for word games and silly questions, Astrid. I do hope you remembered all the necessary details because I won't.

Not with so many people and conversations to keep track of," Millie said as she repeatedly checked her smartwatch. "I might reach my two thousand-step goal with all the walking I'll do! Wait, who am I kidding? I hate walking and prefer to sit in my rocking chair and have my guests come to me, which I see you have practically turned into a throne. I think I shall rather like being queen for a day. Do you suppose you could ask about a microphone? Surely, the school has one somewhere. The janitor who let us in will be on the premises until the conclusion of our event."

With her powder blue chiffon dress with three-quarter sleeves and an elegant sapphire necklace accented with silver and diamonds, Millie looked the part of a classy and welcoming hostess. Only her low-heeled gray shoes hinted at her concession to the passage of time.

"I will see to it immediately," Astrid confirmed.

"Before you go, did you make certain that old Charles and Oswald will sit next to each other?" Millie asked.

"Of course, as per your instructions, and only because I like you. I do not generally include name cards and seat assignments in my list of services," Astrid said.

"Do you know why I want old Charles Pip and

Oswald to sit beside each other?" Millie asked.

"You mentioned they had a falling out, and you want them to be friends again," Astrid said.

"Yes. Have you ever seen them stand in the same circle and have a conversation? When one approaches, the other leaves," Millie explained, waiting for Astrid to take her bait.

"Now that you mention their decided lack of social interaction, I can see what you're saying. I suppose I hadn't thought too much of Mr. Pip's social interactions since he doesn't attend social events, as we previously discussed," Astrid said.

"He used to," Millie said. "Back when we were young, he was the center of pleasant conversations—laughing, telling stories, and dancing an Irish jig when the mood struck him. Oswald was often with him, though he was more tight-lipped. I am not sure what happened, but somehow, they switched roles. The assigned seating is meant to capitalize on their politeness, preventing them from opposing the choice. I'm also placing them next to Crissy Hypo. She works at one of the elementary schools and is a recent addition to the Board of EducationVen."

"Yes, I have met Crissy Hypo several times. I'm assuming that Oswald and Mr. Pip have as opposing views on education as they have on their personal style?" Astrid asked.

"We shall see, and I have not forgotten my promise to Roland," Millie said as she tapped the side of her nose and pointed toward the door. Astrid made a mental note to learn from Millie's years as a gossipmonger and answer a question she had long been pondering: what was the minimal amount of information needed to predict an emotional response in a stressful situation? She supposed it depended on the person.

Within a few minutes, Mr. Pip ambled toward the entrance in a new pair of polished leather lederhosen with delicate silver thread woven into a floral design inspired by roses, a decorative brass buckle, and an Alpine hat. His outfit perfectly blended tradition and sophistication with a light pink shirt, freshly trimmed white mustache, and shined shoes, hailing back to his Bavarian forebearers.

Oswald followed shortly thereafter with his usual quickness of foot and eyes that seemed to observe everything simultaneously. Creating tiny toys required attention to detail and intolerance for imperfections, and his appearance standards were not less stringent. He never deviated from donning a cable knit sweater with big wooden buttons, red horn-rimmed spectacles that magnified his eyes to the onlooker by a factor of ten, and thick gray hair with the blonde of his younger years showing through. He hadn't lost a hair since high school and wore it fashionably coiffed to the left side.

His skin had a dewy look, given his weekly facial, which he only missed if there was an emergency. There was never a wrinkle in his trousers or scuff on his shoe. He laughed easily, almost mimicking a nervous habit, unless he was focused, in which case he laughed not at all.

Astrid was deciding whether Adelaide was baiting her through Millie's disclosures and when she would employ baiting of her own when Harold's arrival brought her back from the edge of the tempting plunge into obsessive thoughts. For better or worse, Harold was unalterably conspicuous in presence and appearance when he entered a fancy function. Watching the news of his arrival pass through the gym was like watching a room full of school children whisper to each other that their teacher brought bags of cheese crackers and gummy snacks.

Astrid heard the exclamations from around the gym as Harold approached her: He's here! I didn't think he would show his face in public so soon. Do you think he will work for the university again? I bet he's been vacationing in an expensive and far-away location. Is he talking to Astrid? Do you think they are dating? Her dress is beautiful. I bet he bought her that dress. How much money can one florist make? My daughter would be a better match.

Astrid is far too independent and strong-willed for him; she's far too independent and strong-willed for anyone. My son tried to ask her on a date once, and she said she didn't have time for crock and foolery. How much money do you think his suit cost? Do you think he talks to Adelaide?

"Hello, Astrid. You are radiant. I've always noticed that shades of purple are your preference for the spring season," Harold said, offering his elbow.

"Do you think it possible that our audience could be more nosey and obvious than we are witnessing right now?"

"Doubtful. They have outdone themselves. But, so long as we pretend we are having the best day of our lives, they will soon lose interest," Astrid said.

"Need we pretend?" Harold said with a wink.

Astrid blushed. "I was wondering if you wouldn't mind helping me finish up the adult Easter egg hunt Millie has planned. She calls it 'Eggs for Our Children.' Notice she did not say 'the children' or 'for children.' 'Our children' elicits much more emotion, don't you agree?"

"Yes, I agree. Millie knows the rules of the game. I would be honored to help. What are the details of the hunt?" Harold asked.

"Each egg placed around the room contains a dollar amount written on a piece of paper, along with a gourmet chocolate from France. The finder opens the egg, keeps the chocolate, and donates the dollar amount to the schools. Some eggs have blank pieces of paper for the finder to write in their own amount. Millie will announce the final sum at the close of the brunch."

"How high are the dollar amounts, and where are the funds to be allocated specifically?" Harold asked.

"They run between hundreds to thousands of dollars, and I have no idea what the funds will be used for, though I am certain I will know soon enough," Astrid said, tilting her head toward the most exciting words in the conversations they passed by; future, hope, refusal, selfish, entitled, and solution.

Astrid was about to smooth her dress and turn on her heel when she presently found herself facing a jacquard pink dress and yellow pinafore-clad Nova. "Hiya, Astrid! It's me! And Jasper! Hiya, Fella! Your eyes don't look so dead anymore. What happened? Did you drink the crystal of life?"

"No, I cannot say I have," replied Harold slowly, unsure of what to say or do around children, much less one who could see through people so clearly.

"Hello, Nova. Nice to see you again, Jasper. What shenanigans are you two pursuing at this moment?" Astrid asked.

"Ba-cluck! Ba-cluck! Candy! Ba-cluck!" said Jasper, wearing khaki pants, suspenders, and a dark blue button-up shirt covered in tiny yellow chicks. He bobbed and tilted as before, scratching at the ground and walking repeatedly into Harold's leg.

"Is there something the matter with this child?" Harold whispered.

"Oh, no. He's off to Chicken Land. Count yourself blessed that they are not having a screaming contest," Astrid said.

"You two must stop talking. We have come to get you! Ms. Hypo is here! It's an emergency! I was super duper a million times polite and asked if she would switch seats with you, and she said she would because she doesn't come to social affairs to sit at a table with her students. So, now, you are at my table, and she is at your table. Thank goodness because we don't like her, do we, Jasper?" Nova asked.

"Nope! My brain switches her off when she starts talking. Ba-cluck!" Jasper replied.

"See? He and me are on the same pages," Nova

133

said.

"Jasper and I," Astrid corrected.

Nova's hair bounced as she spoke, "I am going to tell my teacher that her last name sounds like the shortened version of the word hippopotamus. Did you know that hippos live in groups called 'bloats'? Did you know that their babies are born underwater? Did you know that they are good swimmers? I'm taking swimming lessons, and soon, I will get to move up to the hippo class. I think they should call it the shark class, but my teacher told me I won't be a shark until I become a stronger swimmer. I asked her what makes a strong swimmer, and she said 'practice' just like every other adult I know! Practice, practice, practice. All grownups want kids to do is practice! Maybe I want to play. I can't even play right now because Mr. Pip says I must practice being still, which is pretty much like telling me to practice cutting off my arm. Will you tell him that? He listens to you."

"Let's go over to the table and sit with Mr. Pip," Astrid suggested as she took Nova's hand and weaved her way through the aging group of socialites, chatting about their recent travels, grandchildren, golf, and politics. She exerted all her willpower to focus on walking straight ahead. Each piece of conversation she picked up was as distracting as a cell phone with an obnoxious ringtone.

"My wife and I just returned from Australia where we met . . ."

"Did you hear about the latest news from the capitol building? What kind of world are we living in?"

"We have no choice . . ."

"My grandson found out he . . ."

"I need to get myself a pair of invisible noise-canceling headphones sometime," Astrid whispered to herself. She smiled politely and gave generic salutations until they reached their destination.

"Hi, Mr. Pip! I am happy to see you here. You've done me the kindness of a familiar face in a chaotic environment."

Mr. Pip slowly scanned the room, lifting his hand in acknowledgment and offering a friendly nod every few seconds. "Over half of these people have been my patients at one time or another, and the other half sent their kids to me. I'm glad they all have their teeth," he chuckled before facing the table.

At this juncture, Oswald was escorted by an event usher to his seat directly across from Mr. Pip.

Astrid appreciated the feigned tension that took hold of both men's faces and bodies as they willed themselves to acknowledge the other without making direct eye contact or uttering an entire syllable.

"Hi, Oswald! How is the tiny toy business doing?" Astrid asked, extending a warm handshake.

"Good to see you here, my dear. Business is going just fine. I'm working on a miniature Bavarian doll inspired by Chuckles and his lederhosen over there," Oswald said, pointing a finger at Mr. Pip.

"Astrid, do be so kind as to tell Oswald that he needn't stoop to insults this early in the day and that 'Chuckles' has never been a nickname for this Charles."

Astrid looked between the two men before Oswald replied, "Astrid, do be so kind as to tell Mr. Pippy Pants that no one takes him more seriously than he does himself."

"Hello, good gentleman," came the voice of Millie Rumorous. "I am glad you two have found your seats. Crissy Hypo was supposed to be sitting at this table, but I see she's been displaced by this child."

"My name is Nova, not 'this child,' " Nova said. "If Ms. Hypo sits here, it will be the worst day of my life!" she declared before folding her arms across her body and dropping her head down to hide her face with her hair.

"No matter," Millie went on, eyeing Nova, "I'll just move a few place cards around, and she'll return to your table. I do believe you will both enjoy her immensely."

"I won't," cried Nova, with her little shoulders beginning to shake.

"People are humans, and humans are weird," Jasper said as he hugged Nova.

"Nova, dear child. Whatever is the matter?" Mr. Pip asked, his compassionate eyes communicating his unconditional love.

"Ms. Hypo doesn't like me. You know that! She thinks that I am naughty if all I do is breathe! She won't even listen to what I try to say; she assumes she knows what is happening in my brain! But, Mr. Pip, how would she know? My brain is in my skull, and her brain is in her skull. I asked her that one time, and she told me that she knew all about me and could read me like a book. I told her that there was no way she could read me because she didn't even know my language. Then she started whispering to one of the classroom helpers about trauma. What is trauma, anyway?" Nova asked as Mr. Pip wiped away her tears and congestion with a cloth napkin embroidered with the initials M.R.

"Trauma is a sad experience that wounds our hearts right down to the center. Trauma changes us and alters our view of what we thought the world was like," Mr. Pip explained.

"Like when my mom died? And my dad? Was that trauma?" Nova asked.

Mr. Pip nodded slowly and put his arm around Nova. "Trauma doesn't define who you are. You are not a girl whose parents died. You are Nova Flaherty. Do you know what your first and last name means? Nova means 'new star.' Flaherty is an Irish name that means 'the future belongs to the brave.' So, every time you hear your name, remember that you are a brave new star with a miraculous future."

Astrid listened to the conversation, remembering a similar speech Mr. Pip had given to her when her father died, "Astrid means divinely beautiful." Thankfully, she looked up in time to see Crissy Hypo approaching. Crissy was a woman who was full of figure and frowny-faced. Had she been in the practice of smiling, the habit might have brightened her aspect. She wore expensive jewelry and artificially straight and blonde hair. Straightened curly hair does not have the natural movement of straight hair. No, it simply looks like straightened curly hair.

"Hello, Crissy," Astrid began.

"Harold Braggart, right?" Crissy gushed, ignoring Astrid. "How nice to meet you; I've heard so many wonderful things about your charitable career."

"Nice to meet you, Crissy. I cannot imagine what you could have possibly heard," Harold said as he shook her hand.

"I would love to talk with you about your philanthropic history with the Board of Education," Crissy continued.

"I'm afraid I do not have the history you imagine, nor am I in a position to interfere with such matters. Personal affairs take precedence at the moment, you see?" Harold said, innocently referring to his father. Crissy assumed he was referring to Astrid, whom she turned to and smiled coldly.

"Oh, I see. I do see, Mr. Braggart. Sorry to waste your time," Crissy said.

"No need to apologize, as there was no time wasted. Shall we all take our seats?" Harold suggested as he noticed Nova and Jasper crawling underneath the table.

"I'm sorry to interrupt, but I could not help overhearing the mention of the school board," Millie said, who had not moved herself more than

two steps away. "Crissy, weren't you telling me the other day that the school board is allocating funds to bolster social and emotional learning in our elementary schools? So many children struggle to manage themselves, scoring lower and lower on their tests." She nodded sympathetically before continuing, "You also mentioned increased reports of anxiety and depression, right? What could we do for these kids? Should we have a spontaneous group think tank? What great ideas I have," Millie said with a gleeful clap. "Astrid, did you find a microphone for me?"

"Lottie put one next to the porcelain geese," Astrid pointed out.

Millie clapped again and smiled, coming as close as she could to a spring in her step as she made her way through the tables to the microphone. "Hi, everyone. You know, I am ever so grateful for your attendance, and, like I always say, we might as well get to the point. We have a responsibility towards the children in our community. We must give them greater access to education and lower our expectations so as not to make anyone feel bad. If kids feel bad or ashamed, they cannot be expected to keep going under such incredible hardship. It's cruel! Sure, we survived our hardships, and before us, our ancestors managed to work their way through wars, revolutions, deadly pandemics, depressions, and uncertainty on every hand. Still, our kids cannot be expected to rise to any sort of occasion. Here, we sit in a gym that holds so many fond memories for so many of us. Our kids deserve as good of a life as we had. Here, pass around a microphone so everyone can get a chance to speak."

"What does greater access to education matter if the opportunity is not utilized? The importance of a personal resolution to succeed coupled with strong emotional resilience cannot be overstated. How can one be emotionally resilient if obstacles are removed at every turn?

Let children fail; they will not learn on a thornless path," said Ophelia Payne, the old, wealthy, mercurial owner of most of Doily Dayle's surrounding land.

She had parceled and sold much of the acreage through the years, and though her financial power eclipsed the Braggart Dynasty, she remained in the background of high society, though ever present and ever feared by those wealthy enough to know who she was.

Ophelia was a tall, slender woman with smooth white hair worn in a loosely swept bun. She wore black slacks, a white cardigan with black cuffs, circular emerald earrings, and a matching pendant. Subtle pink lipstick, and cranberry red nails completed her look.

"I do not agree!" Mrs. Duncecap interjected. "True, our parents lived through horrible times, and look what good it did them. How many of us grew up in households where we were told to be quiet, not ask questions, and never discuss or acknowledge feelings? The Silent Treatment Special is free of charge for the next generation and the next. Sure, we all took the next steps to independence, but did we feel loved? Were we full of hope? Or were our homes so unpleasant that escape was preferable?"

"Exactly, Mrs. Duncecap. We don't need to create problems for them; we can solve the ones they do encounter to show them how much we love them," Millie said.

"Give me a break," Oswald said with a derisive laugh. "If you, or we, solve every problem for them, how will they become problem solvers? What? In twenty years, are we to have a room full of executives and policymakers with their parents on speakerphone? Kids must be taught Truth, right from wrong, and the ability to think critically. Let them make their own choices and learn. They cannot learn if we sweep away the consequences for fear of making them mad or sad."

"Good grief, Oswald, come off your high horse. All we are suggesting is that with the ever-increasing rates of anxiety and depression, we must do something to help. Easier access to mental health medications might be a good place to start," Mrs.

Duncecap said.

"If medication were the panacea we claim it to be, we would be the most emotionally resilient nation on earth, so that solution has proven itself ineffective. Maybe honesty would be a great place to start. Life is hard, tragedies happen, and we must do what we do not want to do," Mr. Pip whispered under his breath.

"What was that you said, Charles?" Millie said with a smile. "I thought I saw your mouth move."

"Perhaps sitting in this gymnasium has made me nostalgic, but as I've listened, I cannot help but remember Priscilla Beeswax fighting for equal opportunity library privileges in our college years.

Mrs. Duncecap, you likely recall her crusade more than anyone. She asserted that we could give people equal opportunities. Still, we cannot guarantee equal outcomes since the outcome depends on what a person does with their opportunity," he smiled back.

Mrs. Duncecap's face dropped, "Priscilla Beeswax?"

A flurry of collective memories started flying;

"Priscilla was so kind . . ."

"She was beautiful, and Astrid looks just like

her . . ."

"She could stand up for a cause, but she could not stand up for herself . . ."

"Adelaide hated her more than Mrs. Duncecap ever did . . ."

"Adelaide. Of course, Adelaide would be at the center of a Beeswax death," Astrid said.

"What did you say?" Harold asked, leaning affectionately toward Astrid.

"We need to know how long Adelaide and Priscilla knew each other," she said.

"Agreed. Do you see the expression on Crissy Hypo's face? I spurned her advances, and yet she is angry with you.

Suppose I am as capable and influential as she believes me to be. In that case, she must also acknowledge that I can turn my affections toward anyone I want and stop brooding over the desired affections she will never receive, at least not from me. She's wasting her time and energy."

"You are onto something, Harold!" Astrid said, taking his hand, leaning her head on his shoulder, and sending a smirk in Crissy's direction. "Really? What?" he asked with a smile.

"I'll tell you soon. Right now, you need to give a little speech to prompt Millie to get started with Easter Eggs for Our Children underway, and I will find Mrs. Duncecap," Astrid said.

"Ladies and Gentlemen, if I may be so bold as to interject a thought or two regarding the creation of opportunities for our children, we have a truly extraordinary one before us. As some of you know, the Moose University hockey team is organizing a unique track meet, Race Together, where our talented athletes partner with differently-abled individuals, carrying them on their backs during the races. This event is not just about sports; it's about fostering empathy, inclusion, and mutual respect.

"By participating, our hockey players will gain invaluable lessons in humility and service, recognizing the privilege and gift of their athletic abilities. Simultaneously, those they support will experience the profound joy of being valued and celebrated by their community. This event promises to be a beautiful tapestry of camaraderie and shared joy, reinforcing the message that every member of our youth, regardless of their abilities, is irreplaceable and cherished.

"Imagine the profound impact when all our children, not just those recognized for their extraordinary talents, understand that they are loved, respected, and integral to our community.

This realization will instill a sense of self-worth and belonging far more significant than anything I have heard thus far. To make this experience all it can be, the team needs funds to afford participants every luxury they enjoy as collegiate athletes," Harold said.

"Right, you are, Harold," Millie interrupted. "I was just going to bring Race Together to the forefront of our conversation. Before I explain the rules of Eggs for Our Children, remember, old friends: your support and generosity can turn this vision into a reality, creating a legacy of compassion and unity that will resonate for years to come."

All attendees eagerly nodded, contemplating how much money to donate to such a worthy cause. All played the game, some laughing, some arguing, and by the end of the competitive Easter Eggs for Our Children hunt, the total amount donated reached $300,000, with Ophelia Payne assuming half of the amount. On her piece of paper, she stipulated that 80% of the funds must be allocated to Race Together. In gratitude for her guests' generosity, Millie gifted each one an oversized, glittery plastic Easter egg with a prize inside.

"Nova, Jasper, do you two want to come out from under the table and help me hand out these eggs?" Astrid asked the two children.

Nova's red hair came out first, followed by her

freckled face, Jasper's bare feet, and her Rolly Poley Cove, suspiciously empty and without a lid. "Yes! Yay! I love handing out Easter eggs. I am super duper a million times excited to see what's in my egg! Do you think I'll get a kitten?"

"I want a chicken!" Jasper chimed in.

"If you do get a kitten or a chicken, they will be made of solid milk chocolate," Astrid said as she helped Nova and Jasper to their feet.

"Ahhh! Ahhh! Bugs! Ahhh!" Crissy Hyppo screamed.

Nova turned around, put her hands on her hips, and said, "Ms. Hyppo, you told me there is never any reason to scream, and now you're screaming. Maybe someone should call your mother and say mean things about you since that's what you do to kids."

"Ahh! You terrible, terrible child! Now, everyone can see what I must deal with. See what she did to me? See what happens when you let a child have an inch of freedom? Children must be controlled. Our new curriculum will see to that!" Crissy Hyppo threatened.

Within a moment, she realized what she had said when she met the gaze of Astrid's indignation.

"Well, I never," Astrid gasped. "Though I cannot

say I am surprised given Nova's feelings about school. Perhaps, Crissy Hyppo, the more accurate observation is to see what happens when you treat a child as something instead of someone."

Crissy turned to Harold, "When you are ready to keep company with high-caliber thinkers, let me know. No wonder you have not been seen around town if this is the company you keep. You should be ashamed of yourself!"

"Good day, Crissy," Harold replied coolly.

"A good day, my foot!" Crissy exclaimed before storming toward the exit.

"Nova, what you did was not kind," Mr. Pip scolded as he watched Crissy fuss and fret on her way out, "but, since we are celebrating Easter, all is forgiven, and you can open my Easter egg, too."

"I am super duper a million times excited! This is the best day of my life!" Nova squealed, opening her treasures. She did, indeed, receive a solid milk chocolate kitten and a solid dark chocolate gnome. Jasper got a white chocolate baby chick, and Harold received a variety of artisan chocolates in an elegant box.

When Astrid opened her egg, a vintage envelope sealed with a beeswax seal fell out. She quickly put it under her arm and flitted about, talking and gathering empty eggs. Mr. Pip left shortly thereafter to get the sugar mongers back into the wild of his backyard. Oswald cited his aging bowels as reason enough to leave early, to which no one protested.

Astrid did not need to seek out Mrs. Duncecap as the irritable woman waved her down from across the gym.

"Yoohoo! Astrid Beeswax, hello!"

"Coming, Mrs. Duncecap!" Astrid said, waving back.

"Why do you look so flustered, my dear? And what happened to your face? Are you sleeping well? I've never seen you look so out of sorts," Mrs. Duncecap observed.

"My sleep is adequate, and I likely look flustered because I'm working," Astrid replied.

"Tell me, how long do your longest-living flowers last? Have you grown them in the additives we put in our food? Our food is poisoning and slowly killing us, if you have not noticed," Ms. Duncecap said as she waved her hand across the room. "When I die, don't bother embalming me. I'll be entirely ready for the cardboard box and not a coffin. Who wants to pay an exorbitant amount for a wooden case that will immediately be buried six feet in the ground?"

"Have you considered eating foods that are not filled with preservatives?" Astrid asked.

"Don't be ridiculous. I have no choice in the matter. How much are you charging for your boutonnieres and corsages these days? I hope you have not stooped as low as every other shop around here, raising prices to exploit the customers. Prom will be here before you know it," Mrs. Duncecap said.

"Forty dollars falls into the middle of the bell curve when statistics are applied to floral shop earnings. As an educated woman, I trust that you understand the complexity of economics. As much as I would like to grow and give away flowers for the joy of the process, I have bills to pay," Astrid said.

"And what bills might those be? You are perfectly healthy and live in your mother's house, so I know you don't have rent or a mortgage. Nor do you pay to rent this space because your family owns it. I bet you use most of your earnings to pay for your dresses," Mrs. Duncecap said.

"Mrs. Duncecap, I still find great satisfaction in saying your name. I do not ask you about your finances, and I would appreciate it if you could find it in your philanthropic heart to extend me the same courtesy," Astrid said curtly.

"Alright, alright," Mrs. Duncecap said, brushing her gray hair to the side. "I can see you're having a bad day, which we are all allowed occasionally."

"Are you having a bad day?" Astrid asked.

"I am irritated, yes, and I apologize for my rudeness. Let us put the entire exchange behind us. As a topic of interest, I sent a picture of you to my granddaughter because she always asks what you are wearing. Apparently, there is a Spot Astrid social media profile filled with your ensembles. She wants to know where you found it so she can get one like it for prom, though I must admit I do not care for it, nor do I know why she wants to go. I never went to prom and cannot see why it matters," Ms. Duncecap explained, folding her arms tightly across her chest.

"Golly gee, I don't think I like the thought of being an unknown spectacle for people to pour out mockery and criticisms between a sprinkle of compliments. As for my outfit, Stardust Silhouettes does superior work in quality and appearance. I refused to go to prom, though I would have loved seeing the gowns. Might I ask what it is about my dress that offends you?" Astrid asked.

"Nothing," Mrs. Duncecap said.

"What is in the bitter stew you are brewing?" Astrid asked, taking a seat.

"You know, Astrid. I've always wanted to like you more than I do, not that anything is your fault. Too many decades have passed for a detailed explanation. Still, I will say that seeing the same people as the center of attention and success that I saw in high school and college leaves me feeling like the awkward teenager who lost her best friend," Ms. Duncecap began. "The stories of the intelligence and ingenuity that burst onto the social scene of Doily Dayle in the late 1960s only tell half of the story. The other half is kept quiet."

"Who was your best friend?" Astrid asked.

"*Millie Rumorous* was my best friend until we turned thirteen and she became pretty. Some kids do that, you know, transform from gangly or chubby, with mangled teeth and bad haircuts, into swans. *Millie* will always be too short to be a swan, and her chubbiness has returned, but the advantages she received for being attractive and gregarious are still paying dividends today. It smarts, you know? Not knowing the right thing to say, and when you finally decide what to say, the moment has passed. You wear dresses that remind me of that time, combining the two opened old wounds. My family could never afford such a dress, and I refused to be made fun of by wearing a hand-me-down prom dress, so I didn't go. When I think of my granddaughter in a flattering and expensive ensemble, I think of the many young women without, and my heart hurts for them."

At that moment, Astrid no longer saw Ms. Duncecap as the cranky old lady with unwelcome opinions and unsolicited advice.

Her heart ached for her a bit, knowing how standing on the social outskirts can feel. "Your experience sounds terrible. Were teenagers still donning 1950s fashion in the late 1960s?" she asked in her gentlest voice.

"Not at first, no. But, your *Aunt Priscilla* was in our class and had the same fixation on clothes that you do. Everyone wanted to wear what she wore, say what she said, and look like she looked. Some blondes and brunettes tried dying their hair black, Millie most of all. I don't mean to be rude, but *Priscilla* was a trifle empty-headed and far too vain for my liking. I never understood how your grandparents could raise selfless Aloysius and self-centered *Priscilla*," Mrs. Duncecap admitted.

"I never knew her, so I cannot comment on her character one way or the other. Regardless of what happened, you deserve to be treated with respect and kindness, and I am sorry that was not your experience. What do you know about her library card initiative?" Astrid inquired.

"My dear, you do not need to apologize for what happened long before you were born. Her library card efforts were thinly veiled attempts to puff up her vanity. She wanted others to think she was good rather than being good. Number one, I never saw *Priscilla* do any work. All she did was hover around The Stealthy Picaroon with a steady stream of people coming in and out. Your dad wrote her speeches for her and found people to donate their time. A couple of years later, when I asked if she would donate her time to my cause, she initially said yes. Then, when I expounded upon the details of the prevention of nervous breakdowns, her eyes got wide, she shook her head, told me she was needed elsewhere, and ran in the other direction. Apparently, in her eyes, she was the only one worth helping," Ms. Duncecap explained. "Not a single one of her friends would help me either. I am sure she told them not to, the selfish woman. Again, I don't mean to sound rude, but I was not devastated by her disappearance, though I would never wish anyone harm. I have said too much. She was probably better than I give her credit for. If all people knew about me were the things I shouldn't have said or done, I would be hardly worth remembering. Thanks for listening, Astrid. I'll be in soon to buy some glitter roses."

"I look forward to it," Astrid replied. "We could all stand to think a little bit better of each other."

"Ms. Beeswax?" Ophelia Payne caught Astrid's attention as she stood to resume cleaning.

"Yes? How can I help you?"

"I am Ophelia Payne, and before I go, I must compliment you on your floristry. You do a beautiful job," she said.

"Golly gee, thank you!" Astrid said. "I am glad to have the honor of meeting you. You were so generous toward The Board of Education. Many children will be blessed. I cannot over-emphasize the necessity of quality education. A single book can change the course of a life."

"Indeed, Ms. Beeswax. Lives swing on such small hinges. Good day," Ophelia said, turning around.

"Where might I send you a complimentary bouquet to express my gratitude?" Astrid asked.

"My assistant will call your establishment and leave the address. If you will excuse me, I must pay my respects to Millie. Good day, Ms. Beeswax," Ophelia repeated.

"Good day and goodbye," Astrid replied, listening closely to the exchange between Ophelia and Millie that was taking place near the artfully placed bumblebees.

"Thank you so much for coming, Ophelia. You were so generous—" Millie began, almost bowing in submission.

"See that you never invite me to one of your Easter brunches ever again and see that you derail any

conversation regarding Priscilla Beeswax that may come up, understood? As for Astrid, she seems delightful, if not a bit superfluous, much more interesting and engaging than her nervous aunt ever was. However, I can see that Harold is as mesmerized by Astrid as Frederick was by Priscilla, and I shall be delighted to give Adelaide the up-to-date details of their relationship. They looked *happy* sitting next to each other," Ophelia said.

"You know, I think that might make Adelaide mad," Millie whispered, looking at the ground.

"Why does that matter? Good day, Millie. See that you heed my words," Ophelia said with a smirk and a head held high.

"Oh my!" Astrid giggled.

"What is so funny?" Harold asked, walking up to Astrid with his arms full of flowers.

"More like who, 'who is funny?' And yes, I just had the pleasure of making Ophelia Payne's acquaintance for the first time. How well do you know her? What do you know about her?" Astrid asked.

"I don't know much about her other than I used to call her an old crow when I was younger and would run up and down the stairs yelling 'caw-caw!' To me, she has looked the exact same for over thirty years," Harold said.

"It sounds like Jasper might not be all that odd after all, huh? How often did she frequent the Braggart residence?" Astrid asked.

"Up through sixth or seventh grade, she came often enough that I knew her car, a black Rolls Royce Phantom, but she must have stopped coming at some point," Harold said.

"Or perhaps she came when you were at our house," Astrid offered.

"Perhaps at your house or the hockey rink," Harold agreed.

"Interesting. Well, her assistant is supposed to call me and give me her address so that I can personally deliver a custom bouquet," Astrid said. She almost mentioned the bumblebees but thought better of it.

"You don't need to wait for her assistant. I know where she lives," Harold said.

"I'm coming! I'm coming! When are we going?" Lottie burst in.

"Tomorrow?" Astrid suggested.

"You don't need to close your store for another day. How about tonight? I distinctly remember Ophelia

saying how much she loves late-night drop-in visitors," Harold laughed.

"Excellent idea," Astrid and Lottie agreed in unison.

"We might as well take Oswald and Mr. Pip with us," Harold said. "Oh, wait. Who will watch Nova?"

"Nova can hang out with my mom. They have a great time together," Astrid said.

The plan was forged, all parties were notified, and Harold agreed to drive everyone in a black rental van.

Lost in the excitement of new developments, Astrid almost forgot about the letter that fell out of her Easter egg. She found a moment to open the missive between showering and waiting for her ruby red toenail polish to dry.

To My Darling Astrid,

In the reverie of my cherished recollections, the sight of your youthful form careening up the driveway, brandishing your A+ test proudly persists as one of my favorites.

Your diligent toil remains a beacon of pride since you had to work twice as hard as Roland to know half as much.

Ah, but had you applied the reins of discipline more vigorously to the wild steed of your intellect, you could have invented something groundbreaking, been a professor, or traveled the world. Alas, as all parents must meet with some disappointment, your maternal progenitor and I feel fortunate that your subpar intellectual acumen is all we were required to reconcile.

You are smart, my darling girl, but not as bright as your mother, brother, or myself. Your star in our family constellation is quite pale. Now, I foresee the pall of chagrin descending upon your lovely face as you will surely feel upbraided. Please, go off into your corner, color a picture of a heart while your tears splatter on the lines, or distract yourself by applying glitter to those silly roses. No matter, your frivolity is not so great a sin nor inadequacy that it cannot be helped.

Your Affectionately Disappointed Father,

Aloysius Beeswax

Mr. Pip's Concerns

"Hey there, Pippy Pants," Oswald said cheerfully as he entered Oswald's Tiny Toys.

"Hello, Oswald. I'm here on account of Miss Nova Jane. She has it in her mind that she needs to pre-order her Halloween miniatures, but I told her that she needs to focus on enjoying the time in front of her. All the frantic planning for the next event, season, and birthday makes enjoying the current affair, which was frantically planned for while a different event could have been enjoyed, near impossible. We hope for a future and regret the past while forgetting that a bright future requires a bright today. 'Waiting for permission to be happy,' as I so call it."

"Have you given yourself that permission yet?" Oswald asked.

"How many times can an old man sigh?" Mr. Pip asked.

"Listen, ancient grievances aside, do you have any ideas on our current predicament? I don't know how long our truth spectacles have been missing, and I am hard-pressed to believe they have been missing since way back in the days of The Stealthy Picaroon. As far as I know, Aloysius and I were the ones who closed the safe and the secret entrance for the last time, per our agreement that two people must be present when conducting spectacle-related business."

"How recently do you believe the spectacles were taken?" Oswald asked.

"Did you take them?" Mr. Pip asked. "Before you fly into an outrage, I'm only asking due to the conversation that occurred during Millie's Easter brunch."

"Kids have more information than they can consume in a lifetime at the end of their fingertips. Of what use are our spectacles anymore?" Oswald asked.

"Did you take the spectacles from their case?" Mr. Pip asked.

"How would I get inside The Bee's Knees with Astrid bustling about like the world is on fire?" Oswald asked.

"Did you take the spectacles?" Mr. Pip patiently

asked for the third time.

"No, Pippy Pants. I did not take the glasses," Oswald answered.

"Did you open the safe?" Mr. Pip asked.

"I may or may not have opened the safe recently, but I didn't know where the key to the box was and was in too much of an anxious state to look around. I looked through the blueprints, yes, reminisced about the good old days that weren't that good, imagined what could have happened if Priscilla had loved me like she was supposed to, cried a few tears, put the contents back, and went on my way. And, as I previously stated, what use would our invention be in today's world?"

"How did you keep yourself hidden from Astrid's cameras?" Mr. Pip asked.

"You answer me first, what use would our spectacles be in today's world?"

"Perception," remarked Mr. Pip. "Spectacles have long been associated with intelligence and an enhanced quality of life. Consequently, parents who currently resist allowing their children screentime or impose restrictions on it may readily embrace the notion of equipping their children with educational hardware.

This would afford their offspring the benefits of

technology access while circumventing the detrimental effects of excessive screen engagement on their imagination, self-esteem, and curiosity.

Moreover, integrating a movement feature into these spectacles is entirely feasible, given today's technological advancements. By engineering them to function only during physical activity, concerns regarding sedentary behavior can be effectively mitigated.

Perhaps certain informational content could be unlocked based on achieving specific milestones, such as reaching a certain running distance, completing a set number of push-ups, or spending a designated amount of time walking, among numerous other metrics. This approach could potentially foster a city populated by physically active children, creating the illusion that we are benefiting their well-being when, in truth, we are burdening them with a metaphorical ball and chain.

This will inevitably lead to further educational initiatives in schools aimed at addressing the social and emotional repercussions of excessive screen usage. I recall a Berenstain Bear book that touched upon some of the wider-known problems associated with prolonged screen exposure."

"Do kids read Berenstain Bear books anymore? I'm fairly certain they only read sci-fi and fantasy. In any case, your points seem like you put quite a bit of thought into them. Are you sure you have not been working on your own pair of spectacles these many years?" Oswald asked, unwrapping newly shipped redwood for his tiny toys.

"No, I have not. I have simply spent many years working with children who did not want their teeth cleaned or cavities filled. We started calling plaque 'sugar bugs' to turn their dentist visits into a game. Once they no longer perceived a threat, they willingly complied. I could have made my point in four words: change perception, change behavior," Mr. Pip explained.

"Or, better said, control perception, control behavior. Who could have done it if neither of us took the spectacles and no one else knew about them?" Oswald asked. "I cannot recall anyone who knew about them. I assumed, until now, that Frederick did not apprise Adelaide of our failed attempts to right his mental illness battle. But, if she found out, she would be the first suspect."

"Yes, I came to the same conclusion. Astrid did, too," Mr. Pip said.

"If you came to the same conclusion, why did you ask me if I took them?" Oswald asked, his face turning the color of dried strawberry.

"I wanted to test how easy it would be for someone

to break into The Bee's Knees. If you can do it, anyone can," Mr. Pip said with a sly smile.

"Hah! Doubtful. I am adept at identifying blind spots and using tiny instruments and won many a boyhood battle for lock-picking champion," Oswald said. "Astrid insisted on keeping the deadbolt security system, so here we stand."

"Hello, gentleman," came a familiar voice. "I see you are conspiring against me once more with your treacherous talks of altering my invention."

Oswald and Mr. Pip watched as Frederick Braggart rounded the corner.

Once again, he was conversational and maintained his preference for red plaid shirts and blue jeans.

"Hello, Freddy. How are you?" Mr. Pip said.

"Don't how-are-you-doing me. You know perfectly well how I am doing. My brainchild has been kidnapped, and I will go to the same measures as any other loving father to rescue what is rightfully mine," Frederick said with irritation.

"Oh, come off it, Freddy. You are not the sole inventor of our Truth Spectacles, and you know it. I tire of your arrogance and often wonder what would happen if you could become a pencil that scrawled out sums and algorithms as needed without incurring upon us the agony of watching you find immeasurable joy at the sound of your own voice," Oswald said, his face turning from sun-dried to overripe strawberry.

"How did you get here?" Mr. Pip asked.

"How does one get anywhere? With my own two feet. I must confess that a man is living in Braggart Mansion that I don't know. I almost feel like I can see through the back of his head when he is turned from me into a brain at war with itself, intelligence and ambition on one side and self-loathing and doubt on the other. His face looks like a familiar blur, but sometimes you two chuckleheads look like familiar blurs, so I can't help there. At least I think a man is living in my house. Do one of you want to come by and check?" Frederick asked.

"I am not falling for one of your ridiculous tricks again, Freddy," Oswald said. "What a fine kettle of fish, luring us into your house after your accusing rant about our deceit and treachery."

"Um, I, eh," Frederick's eyes went flat. The lucid moment was gone; his proud shoulders fell forward, and his feet resumed their shuffle.

"We better call Harold," Oswald said.

***

"Hello, Oswald. We are on our way. I just picked up Roland, Lottie, and Astrid," Harold said.

"Hey there, Harold. Your father came to visit me at my toy shop. Pippy Pants is here, too, so we'll have quite the crew," Oswald asked.

"How did he get there?" Astrid asked after Harold hung up the phone.

"I imagine he walked, or someone drove him. If he were conversational, he could have called a taxi," Harold said.

Roland nodded his head and asked, "Are we sure it's safe for him and us to have him along? It might be wise to drop Frederick and me off at your house before the unannounced visit to Ophelia. I won't mind hanging out with him for a few hours. More importantly, I do not want him near Astrid. No offense, Astrid, but every time I see your stitches, I blame myself."

"Very well. If his lucid moment has ended entirely, he will likely fall asleep in the van and sleep for another three or four hours in his bed like last time. That's what his notes from Dr. Sereneheart indicated, anyway. There is plenty of food in the fridge if you are hungry," Harold said.

"In case Frederick wakes up, what does he usually eat?" Roland asked.

"Pickled foods and ice cream," Harold answered, laughing to himself.

 **167**

Ophelia Payne

"Initiate sequence," Astrid said as the Strider van rounded the corner of Ophelia's private estate and drove up the winding gravel driveway flanked by ancient oak trees.

"What sequence are you talking about?" Harold asked.

"No sequence in particular; I have wanted to say those two words for a long time and haven't had the opportunity until now. I would also like to add 'bumptious parvenu' to my vocabulary catalog."

"Dare I ask what a bumptious parvenu is?" Harold asked.

"You asked the question within your question, so here is the answer. A bumptious parvenu is a high-minded, arrogant, ignorant, fussbudget," Astrid explained.

Lottie gave a conspicuous cough before interrupting, "Not to gloss over the importance of your ever-broadening vocabulary, but I have everything equipped as planned, and we get to test out the long-range feature tonight. Wow! Ophelia's house is gorgeous. How have we never been here before?"

Indeed, the view was breathtaking. Amidst the verdant expanse of private countryside full of emerald fields stood a monument to old-money grandeur and opulence—a palatial plantation home that seemed plucked from history yet infused with the vigor of the modern world.

Its exterior presented a striking amalgamation of architectural styles, marrying the classic elegance of Victorian manors with the sleek lines of contemporary design. The imposing facade, fashioned from locally quarried limestone, was imposing and intimidating.

Regal splendor greeted the visitors at the estate's forefront with a grand entrance adorned with fluted columns and ornate cornices. Above, a towering pediment proudly displayed the Payne family crest.

As the members of the Spectacle Circle traversed the perimeter of the manor, they beheld a symphony of architectural delights at every turn. Expansive bay windows framed by intricately carved moldings and Juliet balconies adorned with wrought-iron railings delighted Oswald.

Mr. Pip appreciated the chimneys that rose skyward like sentinels, their brickwork weathered by centuries of use. Decorative corbels and friezes adorned the eaves.

Surrounding the manor, meticulously landscaped gardens unfolded in a riot of color and fragrance. Their manicured lawns, vibrant flower beds, marble statues, and bubbling fountains were almost as grand as Braggart Estates'.

"I can hear the crackling of the fireplaces," Astrid whispered as they approached the front door.

"I knew she got the ears," Oswald said, looking sideways at Mr. Pip, combing his mustache, and adjusting his lederhosen. "But, I assume you already knew?"

***

When a flame is held against the skin, the skin burns. Does it matter if the candleholder had good intentions and a gross misunderstanding of what fire does? Shall they then, in their pride, see the third-degree burn and insist that it was not their fault, that the burn victim's skin should have been fireproof? If they simply understood, then all could have been prevented, and the one holding the candle could continue to hold the candle because they do not know how to do anything else.

How broken must one be to believe the offender is genuinely innocent? Why does holding the offender responsible threaten to make their world built on rickety stilts crumble? Who wants the anxiety of an unsure foundation in the first place? Because familiarity is comfortable and requires no risk. No corrective action. No radical acceptance of things as they are. Thus, fear makes a fool of each victim. Fear of being wrong. Fear of what others will think. Fear of failure. Fear of abandonment. Fear of loneliness. Fear of strength. Fear of potential.

Adelaide knew that if she could keep Frederick afraid of himself by rehearsing his faults, revisiting every mistake, and lecturing him on her superior ability to control her emotions, she could keep him captive. Ophelia taught her how.

Weeks after Pricilla's disappearance, Frederick, at his parents' insistence, attended a party at Ophelia's palatial plantation. She wrote the guest list by hand, inviting only those she deemed worthy of her presence, which she identified through careful interviews with her secretary, Millie Rumorous, who knew the names of every young woman in town. Ophelia only needed to prompt Millie with a question or two before Millie told her everything she knew about everyone she knew.

When Adelaide's name came up, Ophelia was especially interested because in every account there was evidence of gaslighting, emotional manipulation, lack of empathy, exploitation, isolation and control, demanding special treatment, and blaming others. As far as Ophelia was concerned, the only offense Adelaide was guilty of was being too perfect.

The meeting of the two women went as follows.

"Thank you for inviting me, Mrs. Payne," the young Adelaide said nervously as she sat in her assigned seat and absorbed the opulent images that danced around her. Signed original acrylic and watercolor paintings, ornately framed. A black-and-white photo of a stunning young woman from the 1930s caught her eye.

Ophelia gracefully approached her side, "You look like her. You could be just as breathtaking and wealthy if you put your mind to it. Possibly more so if you put your mind to it. But you cannot do it dressed in the local thrift store special. Of course, given the tight student budget you live on, I do not fault you. Instead, I imagine you as a woman capable of greatness, one who can do anything she wants, go anywhere she wants, and buy everything she wants. Own your selfishness proudly, Adelaide. In my estimation, all you need is a wealthy man who can be manipulated. You have everything else."

"And where might I find such a man?" Adelaide inquired.

"I will tell you in a bit. First, you must understand that your power will become unlimited when you cultivate the perfect scapegoat. A perfect scapegoat is a person who is intelligent, ambitious, sensitive, and emotionally reactive. Society as a whole does not like emotional reactions; such displays make them immediately uncomfortable. So, we've developed a perfect system of diagnosing those who cannot stuff down our abuse. We diagnose them with some mental illness that people find horrid, thereby disqualifying their opinion and their perceptions even in their most lucid moments. If, during the stabilization phase that follows their hoped-for psychosis, they cannot recall what happened during the acute mania and distorted reality, you can blame everything on them.

Their sins, your sins, any unpleasant outcome that might suggest they might have words worth listening to can be twisted. How can they refute what you say if they have no memory? Lie to them, lie to yourself. You can even treat them like garbage to their face and deny it just as readily. They will believe you if they are in their most vulnerable state because you've convinced them not to believe themselves. Tell them they have no right to make their decisions. Tell them that you make the call and cite your lack of illness as reason enough, regardless of your utterly inept understanding or education in comparison to theirs. List all your sacrifices on their behalf, and you will be a hero to their helpless mania."

"Don't doctors see through it all?" Adelaide asked.

"If you are the patient, you pay the doctor, do you not?" Ophelia asked.

"Yes," Adelaide asked, catching on quickly.

"If you had a husband who needed help, your combined finances would pay the doctor, correct?" Ophelia asked.

"I suppose so," Adelaide said.

"Don't be daft; you know so. When you have the right amount of funds, you pay the right doctor the right amount of money, and they only see the right things. Do you understand?"

"I do. Are you going to tell me the man you have in mind?" Adelaide asked as greed and envy grew within her."

"Frederick Braggart," Ophelia replied, nodding in his direction.

"Frederick? Is he smart, sensitive, and prone to emotional outbursts?" Adelaide asked.

"Brilliant, tenderhearted, and his parents have spent millions repairing and hiding the collateral damage caused by his outbursts," Ophelia said. "You only need to ask him to dance and whisper 'Priscilla Beeswax' in his ear. The rest will take care of itself. He will marry you, give you an heir to his throne, and throw himself off an emotional cliff to his destruction," Ophelia explained.

"Wasn't Priscilla Beeswax the woman who just went missing?" Adelaide asked.

"You needn't know the details, but I advise you never to mention her name to anyone, especially me. She is far from forgotten, and should her name or image return to social circulation, you will lose what you have gained at his expense," Ophelia explained.

Adelaide followed Ophelia's advice, and the results were as predicted. Within three months, she and Frederick were married in the most elaborate wedding Doily Dayle had ever seen, with a reception that invited people of all socioeconomic statuses.

"Pretend to care about the poor while restricting their knowledge and resources," Ophelia said as her parting piece of advice. "We must cease our public friendship, though I shall visit you privately as necessary. You have work to do, as do I. I know that Frederick was working on a brilliant invention, Truth Spectacles."

"What are they supposed to do?" Adelaide asked.

"Let me worry about that, and I'll let you convince him to finish the blueprints he was working on before they quit the project," Ophelia answered.

"Who else was a part of the project?"

"Three nincompoops: Charles Pip, a student of pediatric dentistry who wears lederhosen; a man named Oswald who tinkers on toys all day; and Aloysius Beeswax, an annoying do-gooder. They are useless to us as their part of the project was complete. Their three brains put together couldn't color a picture properly, much less solve complex problems," Ophelia said.

"What was his relation to Priscilla?"

"Priscilla was his sister. He recently met an artist named Beatrice, whom I am sure he will marry, and they are the type that assumes everyone has good intentions. Neither of them knows deception when they see it, and by the time they realize what is in front of them, it will be too late," Ophelia said.

"Are we evil?" Adelaide asked with considerable trouble pronouncing the last word.

"Not at all. Evil is only an idea imagined by those obsessed with making the world a better place. The world is what it is. There is no good, no evil, and prosperity belongs to those who take it. Everyone else can sit around complaining about their lot in life, as far as I am concerned. I prefer to bend the world to my will." Ophelia said. "Oh, and don't trust anyone except me."

Adelaide emulated Ophelia in every way and worse.

***

"Let her see my face first," Harold said, knocking loud and fast like a little kid trick-or-treating on the enormous door.

"Good evening, Mr. Braggart and Mr. Braggart's friends," said a deep voice from a long, thin shadow resembling Abraham Lincoln.

"Gus? Is that you? Are you still here? I hope your retirement is generous. If anyone deserves it, you do," Harold said, offering his hand and hiding his boyish disappointment at being denied a perfectly good mischief-making opportunity.

"I brought a bouquet for Mrs. Payne. Shall I give them to you, or may I give them to her directly?" Astrid asked, gently pushing Harold to the side with her hip and holding out the filled vase.

"She is in a business meeting, I'm afraid," Gus said.

"I understand. We would be ever so grateful if you could relay our salutations and good wishes," Astrid said.

"Very well, rest assured that she will appreciate your generosity," Gus said as he took the bouquet of deep red ranunculus, variegated red and pink parrot tulips, vibrant white anemones, soft purple and white lilacs, soft pink hellebores, creamy white peonies, eucalyptus, delicate tendrils of ivy arranged in a hand-blown glass vase. Two silver bedazzled bumblebees rested happily amidst the petals.

The Spectacle Circle returned to the Strider van. Harold was disappointed that he didn't get to see Ophelia and was confused by Lottie's gadgets, Astrid's insistence that she change her earrings, and the terse instructions to park at the end of the long street.

"Are you sure that the bees will work this far away?" Astrid asked.

"Can you communicate with someone on the other side of the world? Remember, I am a technological genius even if I like romantic comedies, shopping, and decorating for every possible holiday," Lottie said.

"Very true," Astrid agreed.

The bumblebees' increased range proved impressive in both directions: in the distance from the bumblebees themselves and in their ability to pick up the conversation happening two stories up and one hallway over. What follows is what Astrid heard.

***

"Astrid appears quite smitten with your son, and she is with him. You never told me how beautiful she is up close," Ophelia said to Adelaide.

"Beautiful. Yes, well, infectious bacteria can be beautiful under a microscope, but it's still bacteria," Adelaide said.

"I've seen to it that her brother's pet project is funded. That should please you," Ophelia said.

"And why would that please me?" Adelaide asked.

"Because Race Together will never accomplish what he thinks it will, and I'm sure with your powers of persuasion, you can convince the media to report what we want them to report," Ophelia said.

"Let Roland have his track meet for now. I want Astrid. She destroyed my life, and I shall destroy hers, one mind game at a time, until everything she has lies burned before her in a glorious flame. Fire is the only way to kill a Beeswax, as you well know," Adelaide said.

"Did Priscilla die by fire?" Ophelia asked.

"I know exactly how she died, Ophelia. What if someone were to learn of your story, your secrets," Adelaide asked.

"Your threat borders on pathetic. Did you not sleep well, or do you need a snack?" Ophelia asked.

"Give me the blueprints and the spectacles. You took them out of Priscilla's dead hands. Don't insult my intelligence by denying it," Adelaide threatened.

"You are insulting yourself by your inability to find what you are sure exists, and I have never taken anything out of anyone's dead hands. On the other hand, you cannot make the same claim," Ophelia said.

"I lost my obsession with clean hands long ago, and you would do well to remember that. Remember, you have no more maternal instinct than I do," Adelaide replied.

"Remind me why you are here?" Ophelia said.

"I've been watching The Bee's Knees for quite some time, and I know what you want in that building.

You might want to get it yourself; I can stand watch. Astrid has a rigid schedule, and tomorrow, she hosts Bunco night. Perhaps you can call Millie and see if she needs a substitute," Adelaide said. "You get back what you've lamented giving away all these years, and in exchange, you give me the blueprints and spectacles. Do we have an agreement?" Adelaide asked.

"You are not trustworthy, so why would I believe you?" Ophelia asked.

"I have the picture on my phone," Adelaide answered.

There was a long pause before Ophelia said, "Very well. Before I go, I must know her strengths."

"Her strengths? Did you mean to say weaknesses?" Adelaide asked, confused.

"No, please do not insult me with your ignorance; I haven't the time or patience. You have always been a bit daft, I daresay. When dealing with intelligent, capable, and creative human beings, you must go for their strengths because they are the least likely to be guarded, which means they present a tailor-made weak point," Ophelia explained.

"So, strengths are weaknesses? What if strengths lie in kindness, thoughtfulness, and do-good-ed-ness? How do you turn someone against themselves when they are not holding a weapon in the first place?" Adelaide asked.

"You simply convince them that they are the source of their loved one's pain. Tell them that if they had just been stronger, they could have prevented the suffering. And, because they caused sorrow through their inability to control themselves or a situation that no one could have controlled in the first place, they are worthy of nothing more than servant's quarters, servant's rations, and to look only at a floor or wall. Never in the eye. They may cognitively walk themselves through reality, but once you've caused damage to their heart, they are as good as yours. You've seen the efficacy of my approach for many a year."

At the end of the conversation, three sets of footsteps walked down the hall and the stairs until the sound indicated that they were within feet of Astrid's bouquet.

"Gus, did Astrid deliver this bouquet? It's magnificent!" Ophelia exclaimed.

"Yes, ma'am," Gus answered.

"New rule number one: never accept a bouquet from Astrid!" Adelaide yelled. A sudden crunch was the last sound Astrid heard.

***

Everyone in the Spectacle Circle watched Astrid as her face intermittently relayed disgust and horror.

"What is it? What did you hear?" Lottie asked, taking the earrings out of Astrid's ears.

"Well, my friends. From what Adelaide said, Ophelia killed Priscilla using fire. Adelaide has plans to kill me with fire, and has accused Ophelia of possessing the original blueprints and spectacles. Ophelia apparently has no maternal instincts, and we can count on her attending Bunco tomorrow night. Apparently, something inside The Bee's Knees is of great value to Ophelia, which Adelaide took a picture of. Oh, and before I forget, Adelaide knows about the bumblebees, saw one in the bouquet we delivered, and destroyed it," Astrid reported.

"Wow," Mr. Pip said.

"Can I take a look at those bumblebees?" Oswald asked.

"Oswald! That is hardly an appropriate question at a time like this," Mr. Pip chastised.

"You are correct, sorry. I still want to see one, though," Oswald said.

"What are we going to do about all of this? I think you should close down The Bee's Knees until we can see Adelaide behind bars with our own eyes,"

Harold suggested.

"No. Nothing will stop her. Nothing," Astrid said.

"We're all going to Mama's house."

I want Astrid. She destroyed my life, and I shall destroy hers, one mind game at a time.

Mama's Love and Priscilla's Journal

The Strider van pulled into the Beeswax driveway, and the weary riders made their way inside, welcomed warmly by Beatrice. "Nova and I made chocolate chip cookies while you all were gone. We assumed their warm, gooeyness might be needed tonight. Also, Nova found an old journal belonging to Priscilla that you might be interested in. She started reading it aloud, and I promptly directed her to hand it to me," she said.

"That's wonderful news, Mama, and we could use some good news," Astrid sighed.

"Hello, Mrs. Beeswax. I'm . . ." Harold began.

"All is forgiven, Harold. Come in, please. These walls have not seen you in a long, long time," Beatrice said as she wrapped Harold in a fond embrace.

"Thank you," he said.

"Should we get Roland on speakerphone while we read the journal?" asked Mr. Pip

"Yes, please," Astrid said.

The Spectacle Circle updated Beatrice and Roland with their discoveries, disappointments, and dread.

"How are you feeling, Astrid?" Beatrice asked.

"Can corruption and manipulation run this deep? Have I repeatedly stepped into a trap; winning battles and losing the war? Am I so vain and obtuse that I've brought destruction unintentionally upon those I love? I know Dad would be so disappointed in me if he were here. Mama. Maybe he knew what I would become beforehand and had written corrective letters to try and stop me because I would not listen any other way," Astrid said.

"What letters?" the room asked.

Astrid brought out each letter, written in elegant script, and read the offending words, "Mama, these are written in Dad's handwriting. What other explanation is there? Adelaide didn't know him."

"Your father's handwriting? Astrid, why are you holding onto any of those? Those belong only in a dumpster muddled with rot and putrid decomposition. You and I both know that none of

it is true . . ."

"Well," Astrid hesitated, "who . . ." Astrid began.

"And, whoever went to such great lengths—" Beatrice spoke over her.

"Adelaide," Harold interrupted.

"—to copy your father's handwriting and pinpoint your insecurities is incredibly threatened by you. If you were an ugly, people-pleasing idiot who walks around playing dress-up, then you would be no threat at all. Assuming Adelaide wrote the letters or bribed someone to write them for her, why would she want to reduce you to selfish incompetence?"

"I don't know," Astrid said as she stared at the wall, one tear weaving its way down her left cheek.

"Where do the most powerful and seasoned soldiers get placed in war? You know, the soldiers with the most experience, skills, and leadership?" Beatrice asked.

"Well," Astrid began as she uncrossed and recrossed her legs, "command roles, special forces units, front lines, training roles, and mentoring roles. They must have combat experience, know the enemy's tactics, and be courageous."

"And, if you were to pretend the situation we have at hand is a war between good and evil, and you are on the side of good, where would you put

yourself in the line of listed leadership positions?"
Beatrice pressed.

"I don't know," Astrid said.

"Oh, but I think you do. I think you do. You are not
being arrogant by acknowledging strengths. Be
careful about that tactic, too," Beatrice said.

"Mama, may I add something?" Roland asked.

"Please," Beatrice said, unsuccessfully holding back
her tears.

Roland began, "Astrid, you belong to special forces.
You've been engaged in mental health battles for a
long time, a seasoned veteran with training that
started early. After all, you are my sister and have
spent your entire life supporting me. Now, I will
repeat what you told me years ago: How do you
stand up against a bully over and over and over
again? You push yourself up until you learn to start
fighting back. How do you fight an opponent with
substantially more skill and cunning than you can
imagine? You fortify where he attacks. If he
constantly trips you, learn to jump. If he throws
words in your face, get a shield. If he insults your
intelligence, be wise enough to give him no heed.
Or her, as it were."

"Roland is correct; you are a strength to all of us.
Maybe Priscilla has something more to tell you,"
Beatrice said, handing the old journal to Astrid.

Everyone in the room sniffled and nodded as

Astrid opened the journal and began to read.

***

Dear Diary,

I am annoyed without escape. My thoughts annoy me. My irritability annoys me. Why do words fly out of my mouth, unrestrained? What would happen if I held them in? Would I combust? Would I turn inside myself and break down? I never wanted attention. I didn't ask people to mimic me. I wanted to live out loud without an audience. But their eyes trap me—their disapproving scowls. The dreams, when shared, are shot down to earth with their limited perspective. Sometimes, dreams should not be shared until they have come to fruition. Then, and only then, can one disclose the amount of hard work and dedication required to fail and fail again until you get it right. For those with no imagination and hope, dreams are foolishness and a means for disappointment.

If George Washington lived his life by first listing all that he couldn't do, what he didn't have, and what wasn't possible, nothing would have been possible. In the moment one decides they are defeated, they are. So, be careful with your thoughts. Be careful not to bring down the hopes of others. Cultivate a culture of growth and possibilities.

Now, my dear brother and his friends, Frederick, Charles, and Oswald, are working tirelessly on

what they call Truth Spectacles. I have many concerns that I must bring to their attention, so I shall write my missive below.

My Dear Gentlemen,

As you engage in a battle of ego, I take this moment to lay before you several concerns, some shared, some divergent. Yet, in the calm solitude of reading this missive, I trust you shall arrive at the reasoned conclusion that we, by association, bear a solemn moral burden in the crafting of ocular devices.

Each apprehension I raise shall find its place in orderly succession: the potential for misleading alterations, the insidious transmission of nefarious messages through suggestive influence, the sway upon perception and belief, and lastly, the peril of exacerbating the very affliction we strive to remedy.

Let us contemplate the universal tongue of mathematics. In the hands of a cunning mathematician with sinister intent, truths may be contorted, leading the wearer astray, compelling belief in the inversion of verities despite all empirical evidence to the contrary.

Additionally, let us consider the sting treacherous potency of suggestion when wielded with malice aforethought. Through its insidious machinations, the suggestion may ensnare minds, subdue critical faculties, and coerce individuals into acts diametrically opposed to their nature. Behold the egregious examples of cults and the fabrication of false memories, leading to miscarriages of justice and the erosion of truth.

Furthermore, ponder the malevolence of sowing seeds of doubt within the victim's mind, casting aspersions upon their sanity and corroding their autonomy and confidence.

Equally concerning is the specter of social engineering, wherein malefactors don the guise of trusted authorities, employing honeyed words to coax unsuspecting victims into surrendering their most intimate secrets.

Should these dark arts converge, a dire fate awaits. Certainty shall wane, manipulability burgeon, shame proliferate, and the very fabric of societal order fray as individuals unknowingly relinquish their agency.

Gentlemen, such a prospect is untenable. I, like Frederick, yearn for liberation from our respective demons. Our intentions are noble, yet the jeopardy posed to the innocent, to the children, is too grave to countenance. The spectacles must be destroyed. Failure will not come from forfeiting your genius invention; failure will come if your genius invention indelibly harms humankind.

In earnest entreaty,

Priscilla

I shall report with what attitude my concerns are received. Trouble surrounds us. I hear it. Aloysius hears it, but we operate on frequencies others will never acknowledge because they cannot hear it. Oh, how foolish men are! Perhaps if I organize quotes from historical figures they respect, my concerns will prove, in their eyes, valid and valuable. But I haven't the time!

***"I think I should have liked Aunt Priscilla very much," Astrid said.

"She didn't take the glasses with her when she drove after Frederick that night," Oswald said.

"No, she didn't. Could she have come back to get them?" Mr. Pip asked.

"Were they inside the jewelry box when it was closed for the last time?" Astrid asked.

"We assumed so, though Aloysius was the one who locked the case for the last time," Oswald said.

"Do you think he read Priscilla's journal after her death and later destroyed the glasses?" Harold asked. "It seems like something he would have done."

"Maybe. What do you think is in The Bee's Knees that Ophelia wants so badly?" Roland asked over speakerphone.

"I guess we will know when she gets there. Put her next to Madge. Madge knows how to yank a chain,

and Ophelia may inadvertently let down her guard," Astrid said.

"I will be outside The Bee's Knees with Frederick. Dr. Sereneheart is unavailable, and I do not trust him alone at home," Harold said.

"I'll be watching as well," Roland said.

"I would still like to take a look at your bumblebees," Oswald ventured again.

"Oswald! This is still not the place or time to request access to their private invention!" Mr. Pip said.

"Calm down, Pippy Pants. I have a useful reason," Oswald said.

"I have an extra one in my pocket. Here you are, all bedazzled and fancy," Lottie said, handing Oswald the bumblebee.

"What a fascinating piece of technology. I shall improve upon it immediately," Oswald whispered.

"Oswald!" the Spectacle Circle exlaimed in unison.

The Bunco Game

Millie Rumorous sauntered into The Bee's Knees. "I've done it!"

"What have you done, Millie?" Astrid asked.

"I've re-established the relationship between Mr. Pip and Oswald. I saw Charles willingly enter Oswald's Tiny Toys and start talking. I bustled down a few blocks to pick up my fizzy drink, a cookie, and any new scuttlebutt, and by the time I got back, they were waving goodbye to each other as Charles drove away. See? I knew seating them at the same table during my Easter brunch was a good idea. I can only count once when I have been wrong," Millie explained.

"On what occasion have you been wrong?" Astrid asked.

"You know, the occasion was many years ago now

and included your Aunt Priscilla. I'd forgotten about the occasion until I heard Mrs. Duncecap lamenting to the ladies at The Bloated Solution about her sad years as a misunderstood teenager who wasn't particularly pretty and faded beneath the beauty of Priscilla. When she saw me walk in, she said, 'You can ask her about my pain since she's the one who caused it.' I cannot believe Mrs. Duncecap is hanging onto such grievances after all these years. Surely, by this time, she can see that we have all experienced our share of unfairness. You know, look at me; after years of dieting and fitness, I succumbed to muscular dystrophy. I'm as chubby as a piglet and do not have the physical capacity to walk for miles, dig in my garden, or do much of anything for an extended period. Mrs. Duncecap can do whatever she pleases in that regard. She blames me for turning my back on her in favor of Priscilla, but Mrs. Duncecap was so absorbed in her studies that when I tried to make plans with her, she refused. If you're told no often enough, you find someone who will say yes," Millie explained.

"So, was severing your relationship with Mrs. Duncecap where you went wrong?" asked Astrid.

"In retrospect, I could have handled the situation better, but that's a sixty-something-year-old woman examining the actions of a teenager. No, where I went wrong was thinking that Priscilla had no problems. We all went wrong, and none of us could think beyond ourselves. Because she had two loving parents, beauty, and a brain, we did not suspect that she wrestled with anxiety and depression. Of course, we used words like nervous or feeling blue and assumed they passed like a cloudy day; they come and go, and while not ideal, they were certainly nothing to worry about. Still, I should have seen that something wasn't right. She had a nervous breakdown at the end of our senior year, right after graduation. No one heard from her for months until she started working for your grandma at The Stealthy Picaroon. Most of her male admirers lost interest because she refused to go to most places. Oh, she was happy for people to come to her, but the inside of a chocolate shop can be stifling for co-eds. When she went missing several years later, I felt bad that I had not made the time to visit her. So, I was wrong in my assumption and wrong in letting down a friend in her time of need," Millie said.

"When Priscilla went missing, did you have any suspicions about the responsible party?" Astrid asked.

As Astrid spoke the last word, she looked out the front window to see a slender female figure in a svelte black pencil skirt, a black lantern-sleeve blouse, and the bracelet belonging to her nemesis slowly walk past.

"Careful, Miss Beeswax. Remember my conditions,

and don't pretend you can outsmart me. Leave Priscilla in the past, and I will leave you in the present," Adelaide whispered as she walked past the open door.

"Astrid, are you listening?" Millie asked.

"I am sorry, what did you say?" Astrid asked in response.

"I said that I assumed she skipped town on purpose and found herself a new name and new people. One never knows. I'll see you tonight!"

***

"I'm surprised you are hosting a Bunco night at The Bee's Knees," Lottie said, following Astrid with extra trays of chocolate-covered strawberries.

"Are you?" Astrid asked, glancing over her shoulder with a wink.

"Well, no, and yes. I'm worried that so many people in your space will push you to your limits on top of knowing that Adelaide wants you dead, especially since some women seem as nervous to be around you as you are to be around them," Lottie said.

"If I were hosting Bunco solely to host Bunco, I might be overwhelmed. However, we need information, and I can put my social anxieties on the back burner. If you pay careful attention, you will notice that I've replaced the black-and-white pictures of my parents with the black-and-white picture of Priscilla and Frederick. Someone, usually an uncomfortable someone, walks around looking for amusing items to comment on during these superfluous social engagements intended to help people forget about the stress in their lives while incurring more stress for the introverted among us," Astrid said.

 "Additionally, we have enough food to keep the introverts, extroverts, and ambiverts happy. And why would anyone be nervous about being around me?"

Lottie giggled. "You know why, Astrid? You look as relaxed as an elephant balancing on a circus ball, not to mention how intimidating you are."

"Intimidating? How absurd! Whatever shall I do to seem relaxed and affable?" Astrid inquired with a hint of defensiveness in her voice.

"You would need to be someone else," Lottie said.

"Let the ladies form whatever opinions they may. As for my part, I shall be the picture of grace and curiosity," Astrid said.

"So, how are you going to protect yourself ?" Lottie asked.

"The bumblebees, Lottie Dah," Astrid responded.

"Lottie Dah Beeswax, Astrid. We share the same last name now, remember? How fun is that? Oh! Just look at the food! Maybe we should forget the game and eat instead," Lottie suggested.

"Yes, eat delicious food while women take turns condemning themselves for needing nourishment and then list what they hate about their bodies," Astrid said.

"My suggestion was not a philosophical prompt," Lottie said.

"Nor was my response a philosophical musing," Astrid replied.

"You are getting fussy because you are hungry and anxious, so I freely forgive your crankiness," Lottie said as she skipped toward the entrance to wait for the Bunco players. Astrid examined the spread one more time.

Chocolate-covered strawberries; Meyer lemon pudding; a layered vegetable tart made of pastry crust, zucchini, yellow squash, eggplant, tomatoes, bell peppers, onions, and carrots, seasoned with salt, pepper, and thyme; sourdough rolls; and a charcuterie board with meats, cheeses, dried fruits, nuts, and grapes were artistically arranged along the countertops. Ice water and strawberry lemonade were the beverages of choice.

Before Astrid could ask for the names of the attendees, they started coming in two by two as if The Bee's Knees were Noah's Ark and the food was enough to last forty days and nights. Astrid wore a dress inspired by Niagara Falls. She chose a silver silk chiffon covered with a gentle watercolor stroke pattern in soft shades of blue and turquoise. White flecks added to the waterfall effect, as did the broad white sash, pearl earrings, white peep-toe pumps. A fascinator topped off her ensemble with a dark blue base layered in tiers of silk chiffon, white silk roses and orchids, greenery, and a small turquoise bird perched at the top with glitter on its wings.

"Are you okay?" Roland texted her.

"Anxious. Are you here?" Astrid texted back.

"Yes," Roland answered.

"Adelaide is somewhere outside, wearing black," Astrid returned.

"I see you found a picture of Priscilla and Frederick," Mrs. Duncecap said as she made her way down the food line. "I maintain that your eyes are curious, and hers are scared."

"Who was scared?" said Millie Rumorous as she picked up a paper plate and waited to choose her favorite foods.

Mrs. Duncecap rolled her eyes, "Priscilla's eyes, Mildred."

"I never thought she looked scared," Millie answered.

"You never noticed because your time was consumed with yourself," Mrs. Duncecap said.

"Has anyone heard if Marge and Madge are on their way?" Lottie asked.

"We are here, we are here," said Marge. "No need to get your bee in a bonnet. We are late because we were talking. Look who decided to join us! Ophelia Payne herself has descended from her throne to walk amongst us common folks."

"Welcome to Bunco Night, Ophelia. Please help yourself to some food and find a seat. We are about to get started. Have you played Bunco before? Are you from here? I've never seen you before," Lottie asked.

"No, but I don't suppose it's too hard, and, yes, I have lived in Doily Dayle a long time," Ophelia said.

"You're right; the rules are not too hard. Let's go over them quickly. Bunco is a dice game in which you try to get as many Buncos as possible or

twenty-one points. There are three tables, with four people at each table," Lottie began.

"What's a Bunco? Ophelia asked.

"I'm getting there," Lottie said with a smile. "Each player rolls three dice per turn. If we are on round three and I roll three threes, that's a Bunco, and the round is over. Four players are at each table, and the person across from you is your partner. We take turns rolling the dice and score points by rolling matching numbers to the round being played. For example, if we are on round three, and I roll two threes and one five, I get two points and roll again until I roll no threes. Then, I pass the dice to the next player."

"What if no one rolls a Bunco?" Ophelia asked impatiently.

"In the event of no Buncos, the first partnership to get twenty-one points wins the round. The losers at Table One go down to Table Three, and the winners stay. The winners at tables Two and Three go up to tables One and Two, and the losers stay. We play three sets of six rounds. Any questions?" Lottie asked.

"I'll understand the game when I see it being played and after I eat something," Ophelia said.

Ophelia, Marge, and Madge found their food and

their seats, but not without Ophelia noticing the pictures on the wall. She nearly dropped her plate when she tried to cover her gasp with a cough.

Astrid saw Roland's headlights in the parking lot as she sat next to Kate Indominus, the loving mother of Roland's favorite recruit, Rex. "Hello, Kate. How has your day been?"

"Good enough, I suppose," answered Kate, whose clothes were rumpled and her eyes careworn.

"Roland told me that Rex is working hard and helping him with Race Together," Astrid said, not knowing if that was the right thing to say.

A comment about Rex could lead to a question about his twin sisters who were still battling cancer, and how many times does a mother want to talk about the mortality of her children? Or does talking make the process easier? She'd been sending flowers to the girls every month with stickers and pictures Nova drew.

"Rex has always been a hard worker, and he promised Penny and Isabelle that he would pull them in the 400m race," Kate said with a faint smile before catching her reflection in the mirror. "I cannot believe I came into public looking like this! Look at me! I have flour and who-knows-what on my shirt. Have I truly aged twenty years in less than five?" Kate started pushing the skin around her eyes up and back, trying to make the wrinkles disappear.

Expressions of affection and encouragement given to acquaintances were uncomfortable for Astrid, who was sensitive to tone and timbre. Thankfully, Kate Indominus was a woman who held words of affirmation as precious as a treasure, whether smooth or clunky.

"You're beautiful, Kate. Any mother who loves her children as much as you do has incomparable beauty that cannot be purchased in a tube or as a cream or powder. Wear the proof proudly," Astrid said, questioning again whether her words were too much, too little, offensive, ignorant, non-inclusive, patronizing, condescending, or shame-causing.

"Thank you, Astrid. You are kind to say so. How are you doing? Have you had any further interaction with Harold since that day in his office?" Kate asked.

"Yes, he still comes into The Bee's Knees to pick up his weekly floral arrangement," Astrid began.

"Or to talk with you. Even when he was the worst version of himself, he could not hide his feelings for you," Kate interjected. "I must tell you, he has kept his word to take care of my family to the last detail. He has paid every medical bill and afforded the girls many little luxuries. Most recently, he offered to buy each a wig, which is several hundred dollars apiece. Now that he has lifted the impossibly high financial burden, our family can breathe. Rex can play hockey for the love of the game, finally."

"I am happy to hear that Harold has been as good as he promised," Astrid said as she wrote her name across her Bunco score sheet.

"Don't wait too much longer to decide if he is worth your affection," Kate said with a wink. "Few people work so hard to repair damages when not forced. Harold has a good heart, and you have a good heart."

Astrid blushed her usual flamingo pink. "Yes, yes, he does have a good heart."

"And nice eyes," Kate added.

"Yes, and nice eyes," Astrid agreed as her cheeks flushed a shade darker.

"He gets them from his biological grandmother, you know," Kate said.

"You knew Harold's biological grandmother?" Astrid asked.

"Did I? I still do. She's related to my husband somehow and has grown quite old, quite wealthy,

and quite cranky. I found her picture inside an old family scrapbook." Kate leaned forward and began to whisper. "She had Frederick when she was sixteen years old and gave up her baby against her will."

"Where is she now?" Astrid asked.

Kate nodded toward Ophelia. Astrid raised an eyebrow and mouthed the words, 'Ophelia Payne?'

"Yes, and neither you nor I will acknowledge that we know anything. Of course, she thinks her time as a member of the Indominus family is forgotten, but if you look closely, the eyes give it away. Normally, I wouldn't disclose the information, but with all that you know about the Braggarts, I thought you could use one more piece for your puzzle. There is more to the story; we can talk later," Kate said. "Your Meyer lemon pudding is divine, by the way."

"Ladies!" Lottie's voice rang out. "Are we ready to start? Here we go!" She rang the bell, and the dice started to roll.

"One more thing. I often wondered if Adelaide knew the truth, but I could never decide. The one time I saw them talk to each other was when Adelaide tried to tell Ophelia she couldn't park in her parking spot, and Ophelia told her she would park wherever she wanted. If Adelaide didn't like it, she could call Scotland Yard and submit a complaint. Ophelia said, 'Howling dogs sound like the cries of the tortured, of which you are familiar as you torture whoever is necessary to get what you want.' "

After a few rounds of Bunco, Astrid found herself paired up with Ophelia, with Millie and Madge as the opposing pair. "I see you have a few pictures of the old days when Priscilla was around. I always liked Priscilla, though I cannot say much about Frederick Braggart. His parents didn't like Priscilla because she came from the middle class, and your grandparents did not like Frederick because he was unstable, shall we say," said Ophelia.

"Oh? How well did you know her?" Astrid asked.

"Well enough. I was her piano teacher for quite a few years," Ophelia said.

"You taught piano?" Astrid asked.

"Yes, until more lucrative business opportunities presented themselves," Ophelia said, rolling another round of dice. "Priscilla was in love with the idea of being in love, foolish girl. I gave up on the idea of love when I was very young and have found admittedly enviable success."

"Was the catalyst of your abandonment unrequited love or forbidden?" Astrid asked as she took her turn.

"Tender feelings have never burdened me," Ophelia responded.

"Or they were shut down before your earliest memories," Astrid responded. "I simply refuse to subscribe to the idea that you were born without feelings. At the very least, you have an interest in yourself. And one is only interested in something if that thing will serve them in some way, which will bring them some measure of happiness, at least by their own calculation."

Lottie, who was sitting at the table nearest Astrid, shook her head, chuckled, and laughed. Over the years, she had become accustomed to Astrid's rants on various subjects. She also knew that unless Astrid was seeking information, she often walked away from these encounters, wondering why she could not keep her opinion to herself.

Lottie frequently reminded her that the more one talks, the higher the chance one may say what shouldn't be said. Astrid would irritatingly respond with the assertion that progress would stagnate and understanding disappear if topics are prohibited and the issues allowed are spoken of in such vague terms as to render the participants unable to say anything worth remembering.

Years earlier, Lottie would have replied that

lecturing was not the way to bend an ear, to which Astrid would exclaim that's why she took up listening to other's conversations in the first place, "If I am not part of the conversation, then I can keep my mouth shut more easily!"

As the present conversation with Millie and Ophelia continued, Astrid began asking questions, "Millie, what is your perspective on love, the reasons we marry, and the disregard for feelings as if logic was not enmeshed with feeling?"

"Logic does change depending on topic and culture; I do admit," Millie said with some hesitancy as she watched the body language of her former employer.

"Priscilla Beeswax liked logic," Madge added, giving Astrid a big smile. Madge rarely knew what Astrid was up to but knew she was up to something, and few pastimes gave Madge as much glee as furthering Astrid's cause.

"Oh. And did you know Priscilla? Moodge?" Ophelia asked, glancing sideways at the humbly dressed and adorned woman.

"We were best friends," Madge replied. "And, I should think that the only creature that moos is a cow." The truth was that Madge never had known Priscilla, not even as an acquaintance. Yes, she was aware of her existence as one is aware when another person walks on the same sidewalk, but Madge had no emotional investment whatsoever in who people claimed Priscilla to be.

So, ascertaining correctly that Ophelia's pursed lips indicated her rising irritation, Madge cracked on. "We did everything together, and we knew each other's secrets. I once invited her to show her the new piano my dad had imported from Austria—a Bosendorfer concert grand piano in ebony polish. She was, of course, impressed but admitted that she hated playing the piano."

"Why did she hate playing the piano? I am sure she was exaggerating," Astrid asked, feigning confusion.

"Yes, do tell us why she hated playing the piano. And, after you have given us those details, you can tell us how you squandered your family fortune," Ophelia said.

"I could not repeat her unkind words in public in good conscience, and besides, my family never had a fortune," Madge said, moving her hand as if she were shooing away a fly.

"Then the family fortune bought the piano?" Ophelia asked as her shoulders and voice tightened.

"I promise, you don't want me to say anything,"

Madge said. The rolling of the dice at each table had ceased without Ophelia or Madge's notice.

"On the contrary, I beg you to get on with it. I shall not be a fish on your idiotic hook," Ophelia insisted.

"Well, if you must know, Priscilla said that she had a horrid and selfish teacher who had no tender feelings for anyone other than herself. She said her teacher, who I suppose is you, Ophelia, was so unpleasant because her life had been full of disappointment. She said you had dreamed of wearing a black gown adorned with Swarovski crystals that shimmered under the stage lights, but you had fallen in love and secretly married your expensive and much older teacher and quit practicing, thinking your talent would bridge the gap you made. And, if I remember correctly, you were with child? Was it morning sickness that stopped you from practicing? And he left you? The man first and then the baby? Since you've never mentioned any children, I can only assume that you did not raise the baby?" Madge asked.

The room gasped as embarrassment crept up Ophelia's face. Kate Indominus, not knowing that Madge's made-up story had squared rightly with the truth by coincidence, wondered how anyone knew what nobody knew.

"What kind of hovel did you come from to make

you think that repeating Priscilla's lies was acceptable?" Ophelia asked, standing up slowly.

"You were warned," Millie said meekly.

"Nobody asked you," Ophelia snapped. "Now, ladies of Bunco. Let me set the record straight. Priscilla Beeswax was a spoiled brat who screamed constantly. She sobbed every time she played a song, claiming that the noise was too loud. I had to be harsh with her because she would not listen. We were both traumatized by the experience, myself more so than her. As for the dreams, lover, and baby that she claims I once had, I can assure you that she was merely projecting her experience onto me."

"Who did Priscilla marry, then?" Astrid asked.

"Frederick Braggart, that's who. He cannot remember, and there is no record. Thankfully for him, the marriage ended with her departure.

I do apologize for this unpleasant story, Astrid, as you were so happy to discover that your aunt still exists in Doily Dayle's memory. Sadly, there is often a wide chasm between who people are and who we want them to be. Would you mind pointing me toward the restroom if you could be so kind? Play on without me, please," Ophelia said.

When Ophelia came out of the restroom, all

attention was turned toward the game, and she turned her attention toward Astrid's sanctuary, searching for what Adelaide promised would be there.

*We have enough food to keep the introverts, extroverts,
and ambiverts happy.*

Fire and a Rolls Royce Phantom

The Bunco game ended abruptly when the building next door caught fire and most of the women ran out. Firefighters arrived and extinguished the flames quickly. Lottie helped the traumatized Madge and Marge to their car, each insisting they were okay but walking on shaking legs.

Astrid began cleaning up when she heard a sniffle in the back. Adrenaline surged up her spine, "Is my guest Ophelia or Adelaide?"

"Whatever shall we do, Astrid?" Ophelia called out. "You have what I want, and I cannot find it."

"What are you looking for?" Astrid asked.

"Your grandmother's chocolate dessert recipes. She kept them in a quaint green container. Now, I know you have them as much as I know you heard the conversation between me and Adelaide. Where

are the recipes?"

"A recipe book? Is that all you came for?" Astrid asked.

"That, Astrid, is none of your business," Ophelia said.

"Very well. You may rest assured that I have no more idea as to the whereabouts of the recipes than you do if they are not on the counter in my kitchen. Given that I hear the click-clack of heels coming toward us, I assume Adelaide snuck her way inside, too?" Astrid asked.

As predicted, Adelaide sauntered into Astrid's sanctuary, wearing black pants and a pale pink peplum top patterned with delicate tulips. Atop her head was a fascinator, also pale pink, with silk tulips, greenery, the key to the safe, and two black-and-white pictures torn down the middle and taped back together. Only the wrong halves were taped together. One half was Priscilla's face, and the other Astrid's, both with a check mark angrily drawn in permanent red marker. In one hand was the recipe box, and in the other, a lighter.

Adelaide cackled, "Look at what a day I am having. The two people who are always in my way are in the same room. It appears, Astrid, that despite numerous warnings, your penchant for meddling in matters beyond your comprehension has once again reared its ugly head. You were explicitly instructed to consign Priscilla Beeswax to the annals of history if you had any aspirations of securing your mortality. Yet, in your boundless folly and insatiable appetite for intrigue, you have seen fit to embark upon a fool's errand. Your reckless, self-serving pursuit has ruined yourself, your family, and poor old Ophelia. She can't even run."

"What are you doing?" Ophelia asked, her eyes wide in horror.

"Have I learned all that you taught me yet, teacher?" Adelaide mocked. "During our recent conversation I saw the way your eyes shifted when I said neither of us had any maternal instincts, which I found odd. Then, I found the fact that you did not murder Frederick along with Priscilla even more odd, spectacles aside. You could have hired any genius in the world to finish that project. Finally, I figured out that you are his true mother, Jane Indominus, and even your evil had bounds driven by love."

"And, you, Astrid, you with your—" Adelaide began.

"Please stop talking and get to the point. Are you planning on locking me and Ophelia inside with the force of your geriatric body? Burning The Bee's Knees to the ground and getting away with it?"

Astrid asked.

"Yes! Look at you, putting puzzle pieces together like a champ. Like you heard me say at Ophelia's place, fire is the only way a Beeswax dies. You've always prided yourself on, well, I am not sure what you have to be proud of. Nonetheless, I imagine that a smart girl like you will figure out how your world came crumbling down before you become permanently unconscious," Adelaide said, stepping outside the threshold, closing and locking the door, and clicking her lighter three times.

The chair, the bookshelf, and finally, the art desk caught fire. With a sneer and fake tears she wiped from her dead eyes as she watched Astrid's despair, she said, "I hope you run out of oxygen quickly. Do give my best wishes to Priscilla."

"How foolish I was to believe evil has limits," Ophelia said as she watched the door catch fire.

***

"Well, well, well," Adelaide said as she made her way to the parking lot. "If I am not looking upon my treacherous offspring, I must be looking at a troll. Do you remember those horrid little trolls with the jewels on their belly buttons and the bright hair? They are more useful than you will ever be again." "Hello, Mother. Welcome back to Doily Dayle. I hope you like the changes we have made in your absence," Harold replied.

"Quick question: did you think you could betray me, convince Astrid to fall in love with you, help your father whose insanity ruined my life, discover the Truth Spectacles, and pretend that your life is simple? What do you plan to do next? Marry Astrid and become a family man? She's burning inside if you want to be a hero for once and save her. I'm sure she'll marry you. That slice across her face will be the least of her worries if she lives."

Standing straight, Harold wiped the tears from his eyes and assumed the stoic presence preferred by his mother. "I do not want to hurt you. Please, the police are on their way. Get in their car and be done with it."

"Do you think you can scare me because you are bigger than me? Have your muscles ever intimidated me? I know you, Harold, and you have always had a soft spot. You could never do what needed to be done. You kept your hands as clean as possible to save yourself even though you benefited from everything I did. You still live in my house, don't you? Live off the wealth I built? Yes, you earned money, but only because of me. You wouldn't be alive if it weren't for me. Even now, your life is only spared because I love you. I could have had you poisoned by the cook and run off the road. You could have met with any number of unfortunate events. Don't you want to know how I outsmarted you?" Adelaide asked.

"You're right, Mother. I am bigger than you. It's worth mentioning that I'm also younger and better looking. As for outsmarting me, I am absolutely befuddled," Harold said, checking his watch.

"I see that you are wearing your old baseball cap. You've had that disgusting old thing since you were a teenager, and I hope for once you take my advice and throw it away."

"Wait, did you just admit to seeing someone besides yourself?" Harold asked.

"I have noticed things about you since the day you were born. What, do you want me to play the role of a sentimental maternal figure? Fine. Your eyes crinkle when you smile. You clench your jaw when you are trying to control yourself like you are doing right now. You wake up at 4:40 AM, go to bed at 10:21 PM; drink a horrid green drink every morning; rub your elbows when you get nervous; and you thrive on praise. How do you think I got you to do my bidding for years? People have fawned over your good looks since you were a baby, which I used to my benefit. Your weak spot was, and is, your fear of ending up just like your pathetic father. Look at his room! Charts, graphs, equations, words; it's as if the world's collective knowledge splattered all over the walls and became irreparably incoherent in the process!

"Remember that picture you found, the one of you

two sitting at the table? He hurt you that day and left bruises all down your body. He would scream in a rage, then pick up whatever was nearest to him and throw it at whoever was nearest to him. Except that day, he picked you up."

"Enough!" came an unseen voice.

"Enough of what? To be fair to me, I warned Astrid to leave Priscilla Beeswax in the past, and she refused to listen. That little sphinx challenged me. Of course, we can see where her foolishness got her.

She will be dead as a doornail shortly since I don't see you moving your feet to help. Guess you love yourself more than her," Adelaide taunted.

Harold shook his head with a sad smile. "And so it ends as Astrid would have wanted: with *A Christmas Carol*."

"What did you just say? Repeat yourself," Adelaide demanded.

"Mind! I don't mean to say that I know, of my own knowledge, what there is particularly dead about a doornail," Harold said, quoting from the beloved Charles Dicken's book. "Or what there is particularly dead about Astrid. I think Roland's arm is wrapped around her right now, and someone else has Ophelia. Is that Dad? Is Dad helping his mother?"

"Fred? Hello, Fred! You look so, so . . ." she stammered as the four approached.

"Sane? Lucid? Clear-eyed? Of a sound mind?" Frederick asked.

Adelaide nodded while Harold blinked rapidly, shocked to see his parents talking to each other.

"You may be interested in knowing that I remember why you married me," Frederick said.

"Save your breath with the revelations. You are not going to surprise anyone. I married you for your money," Adelaide said.

"Yes, but I remember how you convinced me to marry you as I was not in the least bit interested in dating anyone. You cornered me at one of the many balls my parents held and told me that you knew what happened to Priscilla, that you knew what I had done," Frederick began. "However, you never said you knew what I had done to Priscilla; I only assumed that was what you were talking about. Since I was completely manic with rage on the night of her disappearance, I assumed I had accidentally killed her. Your statements could both be true with only the suggestion that they are related via context without a legitimate connection. So, you may know any number of things that I did up to that point. I knew you talked to Ophelia, who had a list of grievances against me. You may also have known what happened to Priscilla outside of what I did or did not do; in fact, I am sure you knew exactly what happened to her as you used her pearl necklace as evidence of her demise. She wore that necklace every day," Frederick said.

"See, Harold? Your father only thinks he is lucid, but he is still talking in circles," Adelaide insisted, her lies becoming unbelievable, even to herself.

"Adelaide! You have robbed me of my mind, my health, and my children. Tell me! What happened to Priscilla?" Frederick pleaded as he set Ophelia on a bench.

"Ask Ophelia, your loving mother," Adelaide said.

"What? Ophelia?" Frederick asked.

"I am not telling you anything. Harold, we know you won't let your father hurt me, so I suppose you will be the one stopping him if he loses it again and, I don't know, throws a vase? Is that what happened last time?" Ophelia snickered.

"It is! Isn't this all so fun?" Adelaide asked, pointing to the first responders and scared townspeople moving away from the scene.

"Please stop talking, Adelaide," Harold said.

"Darn it! Have I lost the title of Mother and been demoted to Adelaide? What a pity. Your father's emergency tranquilizer meds are in the kitchen. Let's hope you can get him home before he dislocates your arm or his. Wouldn't want a repeat from all those years ago," Adelaide said as a black Rolls Royce Phantom pulled into the parking lot.

"This is why I prefer to live above common people: all the noise and drama," Ophelia said as she slid into the passenger's seat. "Get in the back, Adelaide. My security detail will keep you contained until you receive appropriate pharmaceutical ministrations for your condition."

"No! I will not," Adelaide screamed desperately, an understanding of what was to come descending upon her.

"Astrid, you're standing close enough to her. Shove her in the car. She will get what she deserves for all she has done to you," Ophelia said sharply.

"If I do that, I am no better than you," Astrid said.

"Fine. Play the part of the benevolent victim if you insist. If she doesn't come with me, a far worse fate awaits her. You choose what happens to her," Ophelia threatened.

"No," Astrid said.

"Very well. Gus, pick her up," Ophelia said.

Harold stood in front of Gus, squaring his large, muscular frame with the aging butler, "Gus, don't. Don't do this. Let Adelaide go to prison."

"Ophelia controls that, too," he whispered, moving Harold to the side with his long, thin hand.

"Can I do nothing? Is this my family?" Harold choked. "Now I know there is no such thing as rock bottom."

Harold and the rest of The Spectacle Circle watched in horror as Gus did what he was told, his eyes sad and tortured, knowing what would happen to him if he did not heed Ophelia.

Adelaide's distress was palpable, and her fearful screams were excruciating to hear, even for those with normal-range hearing. She put up a mighty physical struggle until her legs began losing their strength, and her screams turned to helpless, gasping sobs.

Harold turned around, and Astrid flung her arms around his neck, sobbing into his chest. Lottie ran up and did the same to Roland. Frederick sat down, his eyes turning to black saucers.

The Rolls Royce Phantom drove away as Ophelia waved at the parked police cars, their sirens silent.

Oswald and Mr. Pip, watching from afar, strode forward. "We've made great progress today! I

made the bumblebees mechanical so they can crawl around by command. We sent a few inside when we saw Ophelia's car parked in the shadows, with a window rolled down. The driver never noticed."

"And," Astrid added through sniffles and hiccups, "Ophelia never got what she came for. She wasn't looking for a recipe box but the keys to open the jewelry box that held the spectacles. Lottie put the key ring in her purse and walked them out to Roland before Bunco started," Astrid explained.

"How did you know she wanted the keys?" Mr. Pip asked.

"The initials on one of the keys is J.I. Remember, Harold? You said that the name of Frederick's birth mother was Jane Indominus," Astrid said.

"Yes," Harold said, wiping his cheeks with the palms of his hands.

"What do we do now?" Lottie asked.

"Go to bed," Mr. Pip said.

The Track Meet

"Tomorrow is the track meet!" Nova announced when she entered The Bee's Knees, wearing black joggers covered in splattered paint, a white shirt with tiny pink hearts, and gave each a set of cartoon eyes, a smile or scowl, and a set of legs with high-top tennis shoes. Her flaming red curly hair stuck out in the usual directions, and its contents consisted of writing and drawing implements, silver glitter, two green bows that had fallen out of place and seemed entirely forgotten, and one sad bobby pin.

"Do you know what today's date is?" Astrid asked.

"It's Friday!" Nova said, emptying her snacks into her mouth and spilling half the crackers on the floor.

"Yes, Friday is the day, but do you know today's date?" Astrid asked, more irritated than intended due to the long days of fire cleanup. The damage was minimal, but the smell of smoke permeated everything, including the flowers, and Astrid had closed The Bee's Knees until further notice.

Nope! Can't you ask Roland? He would know," Nova said.

"You're right. I could ask Roland, but then I would deprive you of learning an essential life skill: keeping track of days, dates, and times. How fortuitous that I ordered you a planner a couple of days ago," Astrid said as she brought Nova's new planner to the table. The cover was pale blue, covered in strawberries, and said 'Nova's Planner' in gold letters.

Nova eagerly grabbed Astrid's gift and flipped through the pages, "You got this for me?! Oh, Astrid, it's super duper a million times beautiful! I'm going to draw cute pictures on every page!"

"You may draw a small picture, but a planner is for writing down plans in your best handwriting. You've been working hard to improve your penmanship, and since the same action can serve multiple purposes, you will learn a new skill while practicing an old one," Astrid said. "So, tomorrow, you are to find out the track meet date and write it down. This will necessitate asking someone politely for the information."

"Bbblllhh," Nova mumbled, as she hunched her shoulders, kicked her legs, put her chin on the table, blew out enough air to make her lips vibrate, and rolled her eyes with such exaggeration that she looked as if her entire brain rolled with them.

"Nova, sulking and eye-rolling do not become the young or old, and I won't have you complaining about simple assignments that, if mastered, will allow you to become a capable and productive adult," Astrid said.

"Look, I have a planner just like yours."

"No, you don't! Yours says Astrid, and mine says, Nova, so, they are not the same," Nova said, sticking out her lower lip.

Roland walked in moments later, and Nova pounced on her opportunity to acquire information: "Roland, what is today's *date*?"

"The date is April 12th, and we are almost done with the preparations. I thought I had everything organized, and then little things kept creeping up," Roland said.

"What do people do at track meets?" Nova asked.

"They run races, jump, and throw. The track events include the 100m, 200m, 800m, and 1500m, and the field events include the long jump, triple jump, shot put, and javelin."

"No pole vaulting?" Astrid asked.

"We tried to figure out how to partially mimic the pole vault, but to no avail."

"Darn it! That's my favorite event," Astrid said.

"Remember when you tried it for the first time? You screamed as you went over," Roland laughed.

"Yes, and remember how that was the last time I tried? Since then, I have celebrated the abilities of others, doing what I cannot do. More importantly, do you think it's a good idea for someone to run 1500m with another person on their back?" Astrid asked.

"Pushing or pulling is as good as a piggyback ride. Admittedly, the race might take a good chunk of time, but extending the experience will do the participants good, I imagine," Roland said.

"How can I help?" Nova asked as she shot her hand up, waiting to be called upon.

"Yes, Roland, how can Nova and I help?" Astrid asked.

"Since I refused to use the money Ophelia donated, I am left with volunteers. The team's families have been generous with their time and resources.

While I was well intended in trying to mimic a Moose University experience, it was not the correct approach to meet our goals. If we want the community invested, we must involve the community and the team members in the process. Like bean-to-bar chocolate, you might say. Nova, would you mind taking a shift at one of the snack or water tables?" Roland asked.

"Yes! I am super duper a million times good at giving people water and snacks. What kind of food will there be? Licorice? Potato chips? 'Health' bars that contain more sugar than Mr. Pip's fudge? Gummy snacks? Bananas? Ice cream? Cotton candy? If the decision were up to me, I would choose cotton candy because it reminds me of a floaty cloud. Have you ever sat on a cloud? I wish I could, but Mr. Pip told me clouds are not dense enough to sit on. I asked how he would know because he's never seen every cloud there ever was. How do you think the Egyptians built the pyramids without cranes and other equipment? Obviously, they rode on clouds. It's the only reasonable explanation," Nova said as she shoved chewing gum into her mouth.

Astrid chuckled, and Roland replied, "I'm not sure what the snacks are yet, but when I know, I will let you know."

"Might I recommend a warm drink for spectators? Mornings are often chilly this time of year, and a cup of hot chocolate might help them forget how cold they are."

"I suppose that is where you can help," Roland said.

"Shall I name you head of the beverage committee?"

"You shall," Astrid said.

"Shall, pal, mall, ball, fall, call, stall, tall, doll, gall, shawl, brawl," Nova sang as she began coloring, cutting, taping, and drawing furiously.

"Our dear Nova has entered a creative fervor and will be unavailable for the next thirty to sixty minutes. Would you like to use the time to tell me why your eyes are not smiling?

Roland let out a long, slow breath, "Carlisle is not returning to the ice, and he plans on suing the university for the injury. The lawsuit will lead to an investigation, which will surely throw Harold back into the social fray. Have you talked to him in the last couple of days?" Roland asked.

"No, no, I have not. I don't know what to say," Astrid said as she absent-mindedly touched her hand to the wound on her cheek.

Roland nodded. "Well, I stopped by yesterday, and he was out in the gardens with his dad. He wore an expression I don't like but don't know how to explain. He has been through more than I can imagine. Watching his dad attack you, his mother, who is no mother at all, try to murder you, and then reconciling that those are his parents. I don't know his experience, but I can feel his pain almost as if it were my own. I can feel Carlisle's pain, Lottie's, yours. The blessing feels like a burden; some days, I wish I could sleep it away. However, the pain is not about me, I know that, but the shocking rawness of human suffering seems unfair. I would right every wrong if I could, but inevitably, I lose my temper, as the alum hockey game so horribly illustrates, and become a contributor."

Knowing that any tear-filled response would leave Roland feeling like he was failing, Astrid said, "I love you!" and hugged him so vigorously it threatened to rumple her dress.

About this time, Nova came up for air from her creative storm, jumped off her chair, and ran over to partake of the giant hug, adding to the much-needed support by yelling, "Hugs! I cannot survive without hugs. No one can survive without hugs! This is the best day of my life!"

Hugs without a lecture, an arm around the shoulder without advice, questions left unasked, and speculation left unsaid are the kinds of love that Roland Beeswax needed when being strong felt like a weakness.

***

The day of the Race Together track meet arrived: a vibrant tapestry of athleticism and fun. A bright red oval framed by green fields with lanes marked crisply in white would be the ground on which many hopes were fulfilled and service rendered.

As expected, the morning air chilled the bones, and Astrid, Nova, and Crocus, Astrid's dog, arrived early to set up the beverage station. "As much as I appreciate the faint smell of grass, I must ask why track meets insist on being muddy. Even more puzzling, why do those who aerate the grass insist on leaving the cylinders of compact earth on the field, where they have no other job but to serve as sponges for the inevitable dew?" Astrid whispered, glad she had left her high-heeled shoes behind in favor of raspberry-hued rainboots that stopped just above her ankle. She even left her dress behind and wore denim jeans with a Moose University sweatshirt, her hair in a high ponytail tied with a raspberry-hued bandana.

"Hello, ladies. You both look radiant today," Harold said, carrying collapsable camping chairs and a canopy.

Nova's excitement about helping put up the canopy overcame her and she tripped, bringing the empty cups down with her and landing in the mud.

"Astrid! Why did you pick a spot in the mud? Now I'm all muddy, Crocus is muddy, the cups are

muddy, and the entire day is terribly ruined forever," Nova said, crossing her arms and sticking her cute button nose in the air, feeling justified in her righteous indignation.

Astrid laughed as she leaned down to pick up the cups. "Come, Nova. Help me pick up the cups, and we'll get out some more. I always come prepared with extras when I am assigned to bring items to sporting events. As for the mud, you'll be terribly disappointed to know that track meets are muddy, and since the snack station, the check-in station, the trophy station, and what appears to be a balloon station are occupying all non-grass surfaces, we have done our best. The legs of the table are not sinking, so I consider our set-up a success. Run along and fetch Crocus, who is running away. We shall be ready for our first guest upon your return."

"How much do one of these here drinks cost?" Nova asked.

"They cost nothing and don't say, 'These here drinks,' when 'these' drinks will suffice," Astrid said.

Nova wrinkled her nose and started walking her plum purple corduroy overall-clad self toward Crocus before pausing, "I don't believe you. You've said at least a super duper a million times that to expect something for nothing is ignorant and selfish because everything costs someone something, even if I don't know it. So, how much do the drinks cost?"

Astrid put her hand on her hip and laughed. "Oh, Nova. You are a smart girl. You and I are not charging any of our guests for these beverages, and one of our good friends is covering the cost of the drinks and all the consumable goods here."

"Is it Mr. Pip? Or your mom? Or that funny toy man named Oswald? Or Roland?" Nova asked.

"Never you mind. Go fetch Crocus," Astrid said, smiling at Harold as she turned Nova's shoulders in the proper direction, smiling at the thought of Nova knowing so many generous people.

"Can I throw my water balloons at people yet? I filled them up!" Nova said.

"Absolutely not! Where did you fill those up?" Astrid asked. "Oh, never mind. I prefer ignorance in this situation."

Batches of hockey players started approaching the track with their partners, some in wagons, some in wheelchairs, and others on their backs or in arms. The spectators soon formed a crowd along the main 100m stretch of the track to cheer as the meet got underway. The air buzzed with anticipation and excitement as Astrid heard their many exclamations.

"My daughter has been looking forward to this for weeks."

"I haven't seen my son smile since the accident, but since he started training with Phillip, the light has returned to his eyes."

"Is that Rex Indominus with his twin sisters? You've heard about them, I'm sure. They had quite a medical scare a few weeks back. What a good big brother he is to give his sisters a ride around the track."

"My son told his grandma that he will run in the Olympics. He's been researching Jesse Owens nonstop."

Astrid's favorite sound was Penny and Isabelle giggling and laughing as they pretended that Rex was their unicorn. He even wore a unicorn headband to make them happy.

Jasper had arrived halfway through Race Together and somehow convinced his mother to bring a garbage bag full of stuffies. Nova had convinced Mr. Pip to bring her doll daughters, Lucia and Chrystal, and the other "children" she had had since Christmas. In total, there were seven.

"Nova, Jasper, why are your toys strewn all about?" Astrid asked, laughing.

"They are not toys. Simon the sloth and Janie the axolotl are getting married. Bernard, the raccoon, is the priest, and they have to have all their friends attend. We borrowed some flowers to decorate, just like you do, Astrid. I made a wedding cake for them yesterday that I shoved in Mr. Pip's library bag. He brought the cake without even knowing! He will be so happy to know he helped," Nova nodded confidently, pulling a mushed cake covered in Saran wrap from Mr. Pip's library bag. "Only a little frosting got out. It's okay; he can wash it."

"Ba-Cluck!" Jasper said as he morphed into a chicken.

"I think he is starting to grow on me," Harold said.

"Why would you want someone to grow on you? That's weird," Nova said before screaming as loud as she could for no reason at all.

Harold covered Astrid's ears, and she gave him a big hug. Oswald, Mr. Pip, Roland, and Lottie all enjoyed the track meet for what it was: a community of people taking care of one another, all equal in the eyes of each other. And, if not all, then at least for one day, most.

Astrid saw Ophelia's Rolls Royce Phantom drive by and heard her say, "I'm visiting relatives for the summer. I'll call you when I get back."

Jasper transformed into a chicken.

If you are reading this page, I presumptuously assume you want to read more of Astrid and the eccentric cast of Doily Dayle. Enjoy!

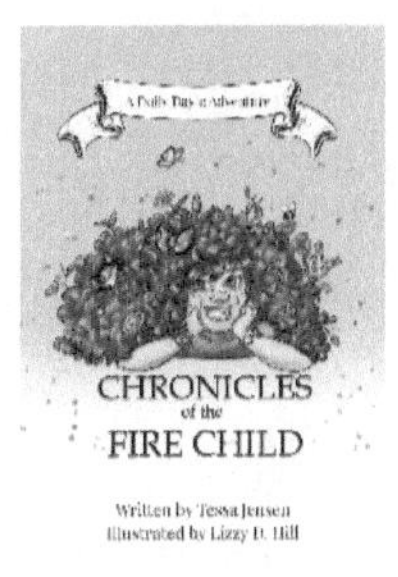

Before the sunshine, there was a heavy storm. Read my memoir to discover how Jesus Christ transformed my broken and bitter life into one of joy and peace.

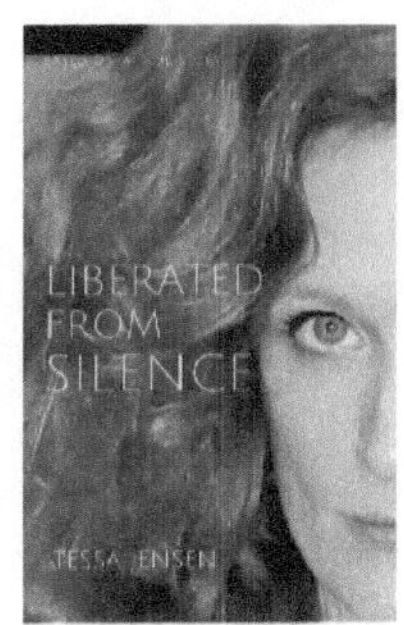

About the Author

Tessa Jensen lives in the Pacific Northwest with her husband, four children, two dogs, and a cat. Their home is bursting with vivid imaginations, laughter, an occasional clash of opinions, and such a cacophony of noise that they are under investigation for noise pollution infringements.

Tessa earned a Bachelor of Science in Public Health from BYU-Idaho and has been practicing massage therapy for over a decade and distance running for over two decades. She loves Jesus, her family, and her friends, talking, crafting, baking, and making others laugh. Astrid Beeswax, The Venom, is the second book in her Astrid Beeswax series.

Follow Tessa

tessa-jensen.com

@tessasjensen

About the Illustrator

Lizzy D. Hill grew up on a farm in Southern Idaho, where she was free to explore the world around her and find the enchanting things in it. She enjoys fantasy books, researching fashion, exploring nature, and especially listening to music.

Music sets her imagination off so much that most of her art is inspired by various songs and the stories she sees as she listens to them. To pursue these inspirations, Lizzy D. got an Associate of Fine Arts at BYU-Idaho and has been displaying her whimsical art at Science Fiction and Fantasy conventions and various stores and shops. She also had a successful Kickstarter for her coloring book Wickedly Whimsical Witches and has illustrated children's books in recent years. She is happily married to her best friend and living in Washington State with their son and noisy blue-eyed kitty.

Follow Lizzy

lizzydart.com

@lizzydhill